THE
DICK TRACY
CASEBOOK

THE DICK TRACY CASEBOOK

Favorite Adventures, 1931-1990

Selected by

Max Allan Collins and Dick Locher

ST. MARTIN'S PRESS   NEW YORK

The editors wish to thank Matt Masterson, Dick Tracy's #1 fan, for his generous assistance with this volume.

Editor: Stuart Moore
Managing Editor: Amelie Littell
Design by Glen M. Edelstein

Library of Congress Cataloging-in-Publication Data

The Dick Tracy casebook : favorite adventures, 1931–1990 / selected by
  Max Allan Collins & Dick Locher.
      p.   cm.
    ISBN 0-312-04461-5 (deluxe) — ISBN 0-312-04462-3 (pbk.)
    1. Gould, Chester. Dick Tracy. I. Collins, Max Allan.
  II. Locher, Dick III. Dick Tracy (Comic strip)
  PN6728.D53D534   1990
  741.5'0973—dc20   89-70359
                                                   CIP

First Edition
10 9 8 7 6 5 4 3 2 1

CONTENTS

INTRODUCTION

I remember a conversation with my father, many years back. It was on one of our special father-son fishing trips. He said to me, "You know, I grew up in the golden age of everything!"

I was taken aback. I knew that his years were the years of America's great Depression. "C'mon, Dad, how could it have been the golden years when there was joblessness, hunger, suffering, and loss of purpose in the country?"

"That's just it—Americans were desperate. They wanted work! They worked furiously to keep whatever they had and I figure they made the best of everything just to hang on."

I had no idea where my dad was going with this, but I listened intently because my father had some sly observations on life. "Analyze it," he said. "We had the golden age of sports, the golden age of movies, automobiles, literature, and aviation. We had the Lou Gehrigs, Babe Ruths, the Cords, and Duesenbergs, Clark Gable, Jimmy Doolittle, Hemingway, and F. Scott Fitzgerald."

My father continued, "I don't think we recognized it then, but it was the golden age. If we could sidestep the suffering I mentioned, it was a high point in America's acknowledgment of quality and pride. It was America's renaissance." I nodded approvingly. My father was all wise.

As I think about my father's words today, I would have added one more category to his list. His youth was the golden age of cartooning.

In the 1920s and 1930s, giants reigned in the comic industry. I'm sure you remember *Krazy Kat*, *Li'l Abner*, *Terry and the Pirates*, and *Buck Rogers*. It's a world in which I am deeply immersed, for . . . I draw *Dick Tracy*.

I was asked to become Chester Gould's assistant in the late 1950s, and I had the opportunity to observe and admire the workings of one of the true masters of the golden age of comics. I watched his drawing unfold. I saw his kaleidoscope of villains come and then go to their untimely demises. In the likes of B.O. Plenty and Gravel Gertie, I saw humor as it had

never been delivered before. I heard people call to see what would happen to Tracy because they couldn't wait till his "Perils of Pauline" type of adventure came to a conclusion.

Today, America's comic pages are not the same. In some ways they are better. The pages of our newspapers now have more gag-type strips. Who, today, could not smile with Charlie Brown and his clan, the everyday traumas of *For Better or for Worse*, with Calvin the mischievous, or *Hagar the Horrible*? These are classics in their own right.

However, we still retain a cord to the past. We have comics today born of dedication and inspiration—strips that have such entertainment value that they still flourish. *Orphan Annie* and *Dick Tracy* are two of these strips. They continue to enhance the comic pages because they possess a key ingredient of today's popular strips—humor.

When Chet needed me, I agreed to do the strip because I was fond of him. When I worked with him on *Tracy* he insisted on using a humorous tone from time to time. It wasn't all blood and guts. He did this because he possessed a fine sense of humor of his own. I can remember vividly one practical joke that he took great delight in executing.

One Friday evening we were finishing up a week's worth of the Tracy strip. Chet asked me to draw a machine gun in panel three of the Sunday page. Since it was late in the day, he suggested that I take it home to finish it up, and—in keeping with his policy of strict authenticity—that I use a machine gun I would find on the top shelf of our closet. "Wrap it up and take it home," he said as he stepped out the door.

I investigated, with the help of a stool, and, sure enough, there on the shelf—way back behind some paper supplies—was a true-to-life German Schmeisser, a World War II machine gun. I rolled it in brown kraft paper and, with my drawing case and strips, started out the door of the Tribune Tower to catch my 5:40 train at Union Station, a mile away.

I wasn't twenty feet out the door when I heard a stern voice say, "Sir, may I speak with

you?" I glimpsed a figure out of the corner of my eye. It was one of Chicago's finest. I thought, "My God, I'm carrying a machine gun and a Chicago policeman wants to converse!" My first reaction was to quicken the pace and put some distance between us.

A hand on my shoulder destroyed that notion immediately. As he stared into my frightened face, the policeman said, "Would you step over to my squad car, please!" Panic had now set in. I would never see my wife and son again, except in Joliet prison. I was carrying an automatic weapon through the streets of Chicago—and the police knew it! "What have you got in the package?" the cop asked, gently seating me in the back of his blue-and-white police cruiser.

"Leftover pizza," was the best I could come up with, as sweat appeared all over my body.

"Let's see the pizza!" came a firm reply.

"Now wait a minute, Officer, there's a story behind this. . . ." I unwrapped the blue-steel instrument of destruction.

"I know there is," the cop replied. "Chester Gould called us and told us to give you a ride to Union Station!"

I call this mega-humor. Chet could make anyone laugh—including Chicago cops.

The Dick Tracy strip continued after Chet retired. It was handed down to two exceptional comic strip practitioners, Max Allan Collins and Rick Fletcher. The humor remained, as well as sparkling art, and Tracy was catapulted into new adventures.

Life sometimes imitates art, where personalities come and go. The strip suddenly lost its artist when Rick Fletcher died. I was called in to take his place. A challenge, to be sure. There had been many Tracy scenarios since I'd last worked with Chet, but Allan and I forged ahead.

I was elated at this point to be joined by my son John, who had just completed his art studies at Northern Illinois University. The three of us took Tracy into some uncharted waters with great gusto. We toyed with toxic wastes and cryogenics, and schemed with the KGB, sending Tracy to the Soviet Union.

But just as suddenly as before, we lost another Tracy man—John. I grieved for many reasons, but losing someone so close, who I had thought would some day do Tracy, haunts me today.

Many of America's strips are gone now—gone like the Clark Gables, the Humphrey Bogarts, the Packards and the Auburns. Can we see their likes now? Can we see the Li'l Abners, Offissa Pupp, Pruneface, B-B Eyes, Pat Ryan, and Terry? Not really, but then maybe we don't have to. . . . I still remember the best, as did my father. It truly was a unique age of everything. He was right, and he was lucky.

Let's hope the generations of today start their own list of greats. I have mine and I revel in them. My son, Steve, and his son, Michael, have theirs, and they are great. I can hear them now: "Dad, did you see what Putty Puss did today?" And I know some things are still golden.

DICK LOCHER

THE 1930s
THE HOTEL MURDERS
by Chester Gould
3/9/36–4/27/36

Chester Gould introduced his square-jawed sleuth in late 1931, causing a sensation in the comic-strip world. While soap-opera continuities such as Harold Grey's *Little Orphan Annie* and Sidney Smith's *The Gumps* preceded *Dick Tracy*, as did a few adventure strips (notably Roy Crane's *Wash Tubbs* and Hal Foster's *Tarzan*), it was *Tracy* that set the tone and the standard for fast-paced, violently melodramatic story-strip fare.

In the opening days of the strip, the murder of Tess Trueheart's father by minions of the Al Capone-like Big Boy led to Tracy swearing vengeance and joining the police force of a major unnamed city that might be Chicago. His single-minded, meet-violence-with-violence war on crime continues unabated to this day.

That the first villain, Big Boy, was patterned on Capone is of course no accident; Gould, a Chicagoan (by way of Oklahoma), shared the frustration of the local citizenry when Capone brazenly shot down reporter Jake Lingle (who proved to be dirty himself, but never mind) and apparently ordained the brutal St. Valentine's Day massacre. Partially inspired by the publicized successes of a handful of federal men (notably the young, handsome Eliot Ness), Gould—by instinct a "bigfoot" humor cartoonist—turned his pen to the creation of a modern-day American Sherlock Holmes who might take on the Capones of the urban jungle.

Gould patterned Tracy rather directly on Holmes, a snap-brim fedora substituting for the deerstalker cap, the yellow topcoat taking the place of the Inverness cape, and a loyal but not brilliant Watson in Pat Patton (replaced later by the more street-smart Sam Catchem). But Gould mixed realism with his fantasy; he was always concerned with matters of police procedure and criminology—lie detectors, ballistic tests, and fingerprints were part of Tracy's police-science arsenal from day one.

In the 1930s, Tracy most frequently fought villains who might have crawled off the front page: Big Boy was Capone, Boris Arson escaped jail in a Dillinger-like fashion, and other Gould baddies invoked Bonnie and Clyde, Baby-Face Nelson, Legs Diamond, and other outlaws and gangsters of the day. Movie stars provided the pattern for some characters: Edward G. Robinson inspired both Stooge Viller and Dan Mucelli; Marlene Dietrich was Marrow; Boris Karloff was Karpse. Larger-than-life villains like Flattop and the Brow were not yet part of Tracy's world.

Also characterizing the thirties *Tracy* was a strong element of soap opera, always present in the strip (even today) but never more so than during the Depression years. Much of this derived from Tracy's ongoing, sometimes stormy relationship with his fiancée Tess Trueheart; but drama also characterized Tracy's relationship with his adoptive son Junior, whose dead-end kid background provided heartache, particularly when his real parents turned up. Sequences in hospitals, where sympathetic characters fight for their lives (and sometimes lose) while Tracy and others pray for their recovery, are common throughout the run of the strip.

"The Hotel Murders" is a rarity in *Dick Tracy*—a mystery. Tracy, America's most famous fictional detective, has hardly ever tackled mysteries in the true Agatha Christie/Ellery Queen or even Hammett/Chandler sense. The day-to-day nature of story strips, with continuities lasting months, makes it difficult if not impossible for readers to keep track of clues, red herrings, and the various details necessary to keep a whodunit afloat. (The only other whodunit to appear in Tracy was a 1982–83 Collins/Fletcher continuity, reprinted in 1987 by Dragon Lady Press as "Who Shot Pat Patton?") Consequently, this is a short continuity, by Gould standards. But the solution is a memorable one, and would be prominently referred to, decades later, in the Sydney Pollack/Robert Redford film *Three Days of the Condor*.

This tale is also unusual in that the perpetrator is sympathetic; Gould rarely had sympathy for his bad guys, despite his uncanny ability to make even the most evil villains interesting and human.

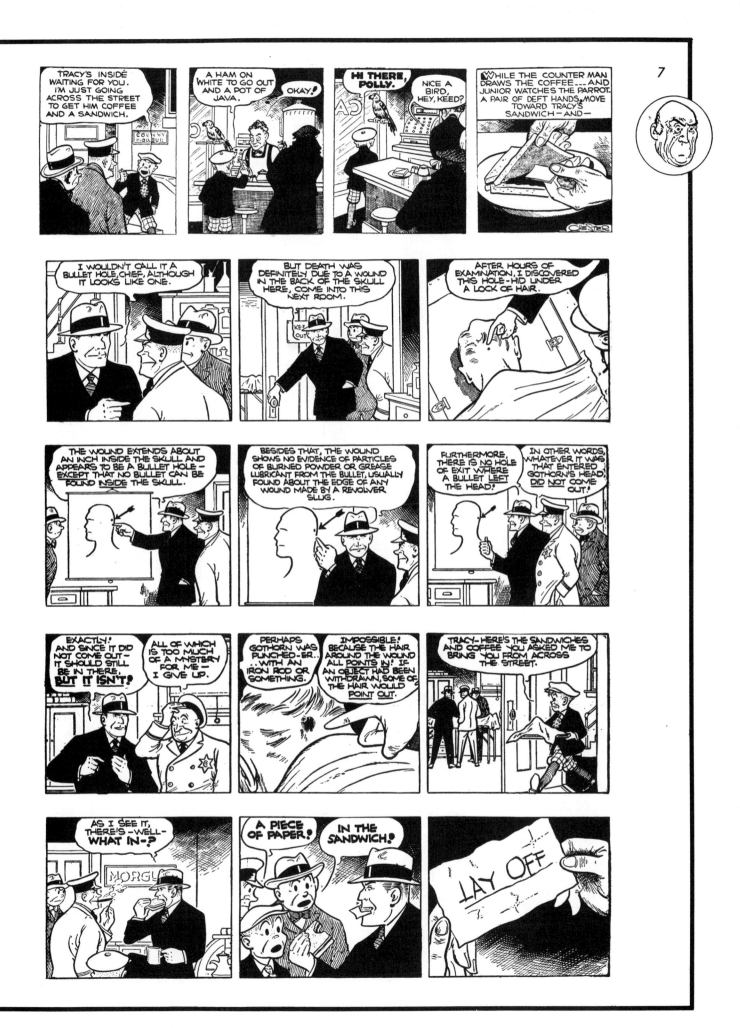

THE 1940s
THE BROW
by Chester Gould
5/22/44–9/26/44

As the outlaw era of Dillinger, Bonnie and Clyde, and Baby-Face Nelson drew to a close, and as organized crime began to shun publicity and retreat behind respectable fronts, newspaper headlines were filled with a new kind of "gangster," a larger-than-life international villain who robbed not banks but entire countries, who didn't kidnap individuals but occupied nations.

Gould always saw himself in competition with the front page, and when Hitler and Mussolini rose to power, *Dick Tracy*'s creator upped the home-grown criminal ante. A succession of vivid grotesques, their names often echoing their physiognomies, began squaring off with Tracy, and in 1941 the first two of the great "crazy villains" appeared: Little Face Finny and the Mole. In 1942 and '43, B-B Eyes, Pruneface, and 88 Keyes joined the ever-growing Rogues' Gallery.

By just about any critical yardstick, however, 1944 was Gould's golden year. During a time of personal problems—his beloved wife Edna was ill during this period—Gould threw himself into his work and came up with three of his most enduring villains in one blazing twelve-month run: Flattop, the Brow, and Shaky.

As popular as Tracy was throughout the thirties (spinning off into toys, radio series, and movie serials), the 1940s—with 1944 the point of critical mass—were the pinnacle. Radio comedians included *Tracy* references in their gags; Daffy Duck parodied the shovel-jawed sleuth as "Duck Twacy" in *The Great Piggy Bank Robbery*; a new series of feature films was launched at RKO. Gould was at his creative peak, and not just in the villainy department: B.O. Plenty, Gravel Gertie, Sparkle Plenty, Vitamin Flintheart, and Diet Smith all made their first appearances in the 1940s.

With the exception of "leetle" Sparkle, that listing of sympathetic characters must be clarified: both Vitamin and Diet came aboard under somewhat suspicious circumstances; and the lovable, rustic hillbilly characters B.O. Plenty and Gravel Gertie—comic creations that harked back to Gould's "big-foot" roots—entered, essentially, as villains.

Gertie, in fact, makes her entrance in this story—not so much as a villain, but as an eccentric soul, a physical witch with a heavenly voice (a typical Gould irony) who aids and abets the Brow.

And though the Brow may not have quite achieved the household name status of Flattop, Pruneface, and the Mole, he is inarguably the quintessential Gould grotesque villain. Physically hideous yet sauve, sadistic yet capable of love, the Brow is a Nazi spy whose cunning, whose unending resourcefulness, whose twisted courage allows him to lead Tracy on a grand extended chase reminiscent of the outlaw days of Bonnie and Clyde.

Also memorable are the Summer Sisters, who are not bad girls, really—more like naughty. What becomes of them is a lesson in Gould morality (more of this in the Afterword; we don't want to spoil one of Gould's greatest yarns).

"The Case of the Brow" (as a 1946 reprint volume dubbed it) was gathered in *The Celebrated Cases of Dick Tracy* (Chelsea House, 1970). The editors of this volume have tried to avoid using much-reprinted stories here, but (a) we are assembling personal favorites and the Brow falls into that category for both editors, and (b) in *Celebrated Cases*, the Brow tale was savagely edited (the Sunday pages were omitted) and the brutal ending was censored. As you will see, the fate this Nazi spy meets represents Gould at his most pointedly ironic.

Since it has been over forty years since the complete Brow story was collected, we are proud to present here what may well be the best tale from Gould's finest year.

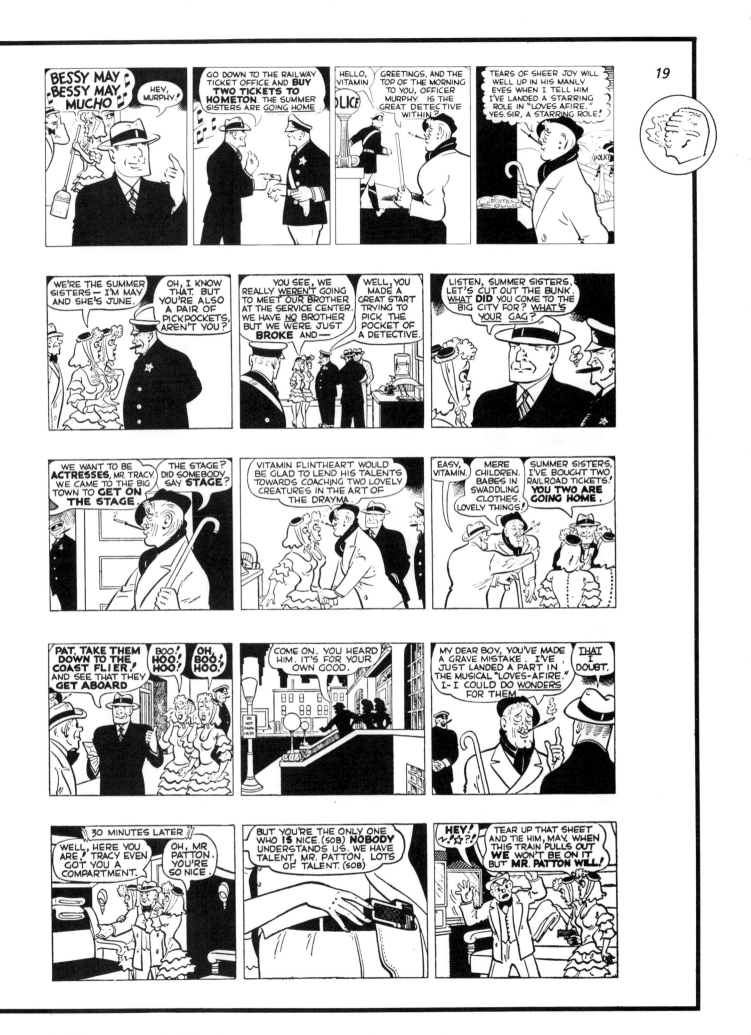

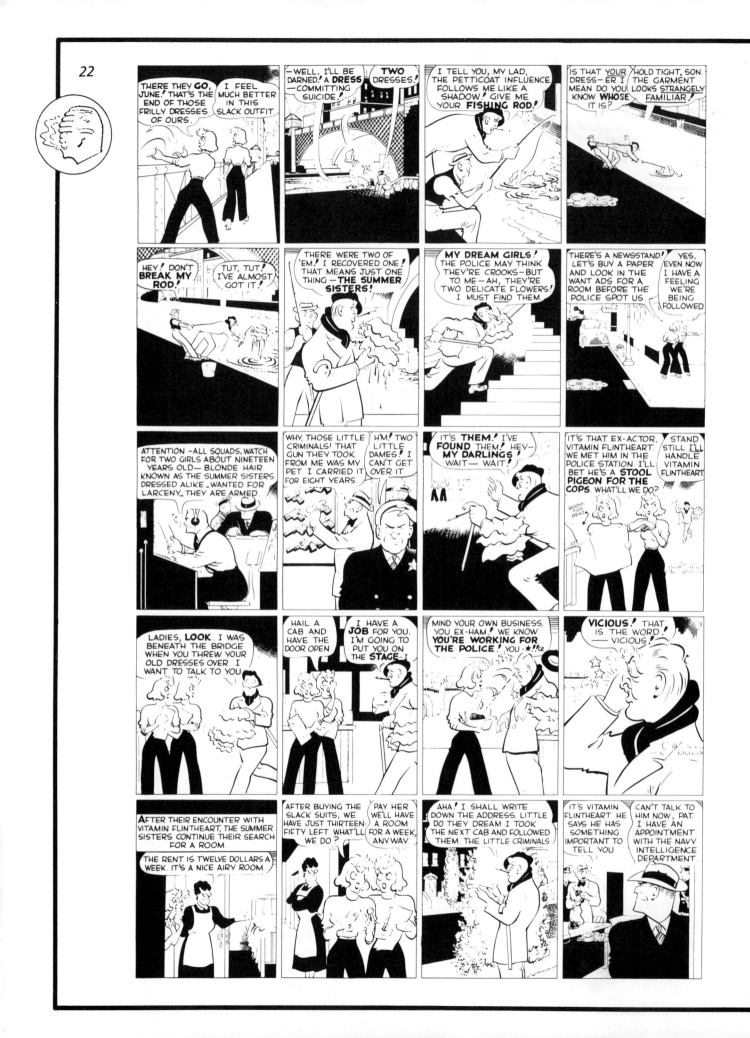

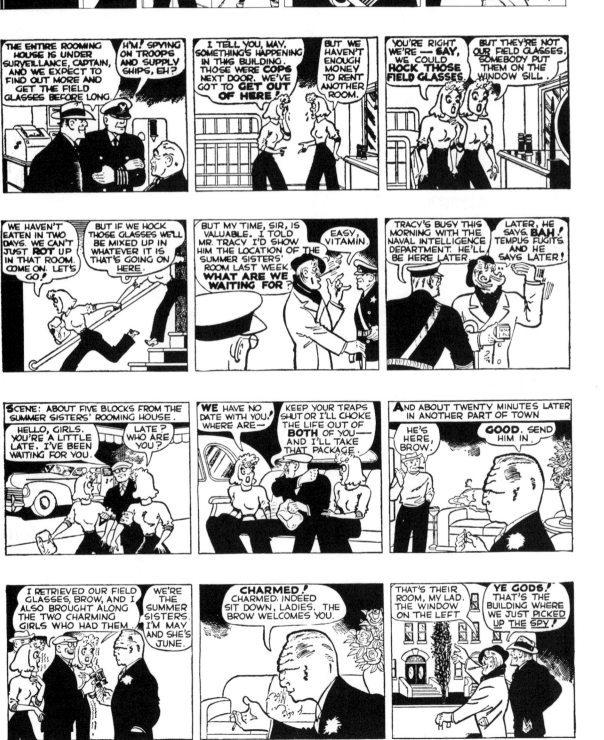

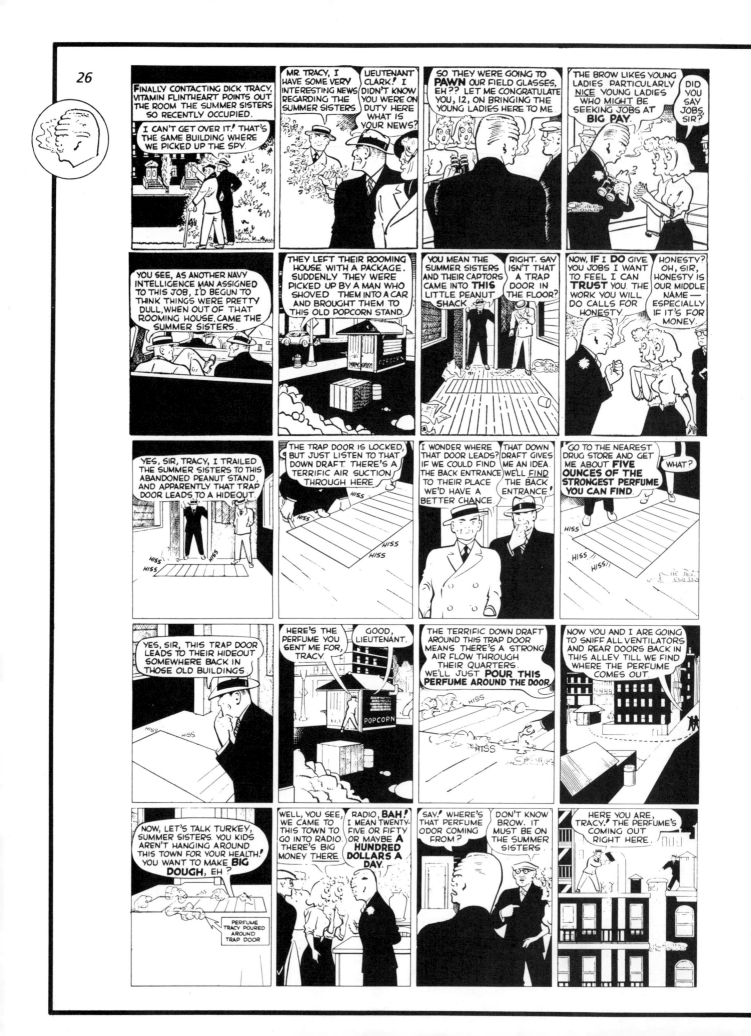

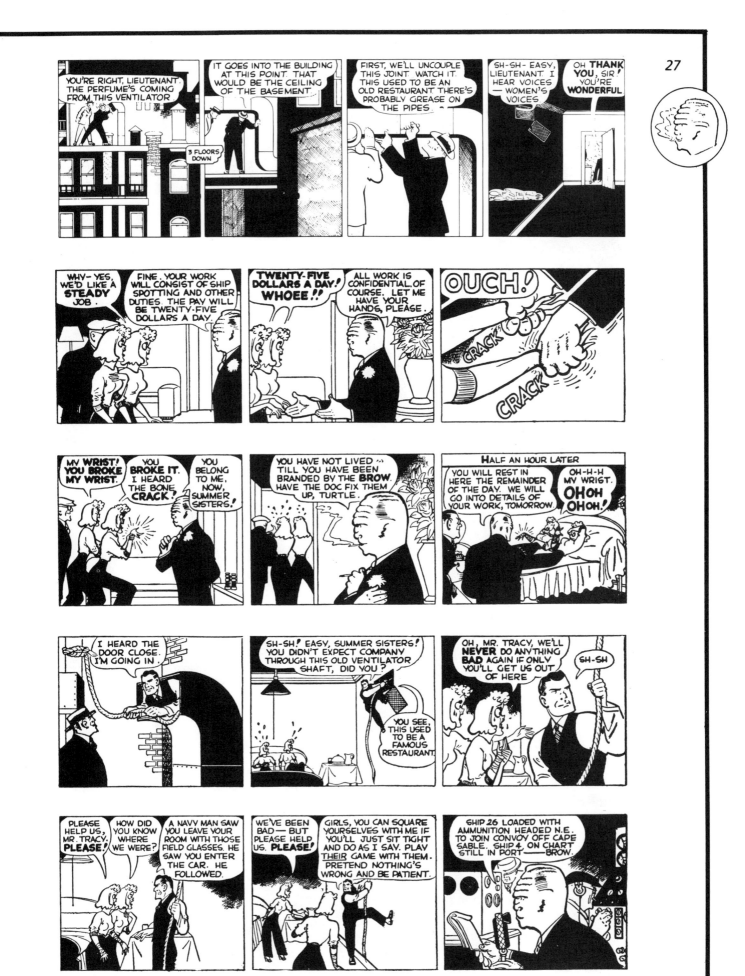

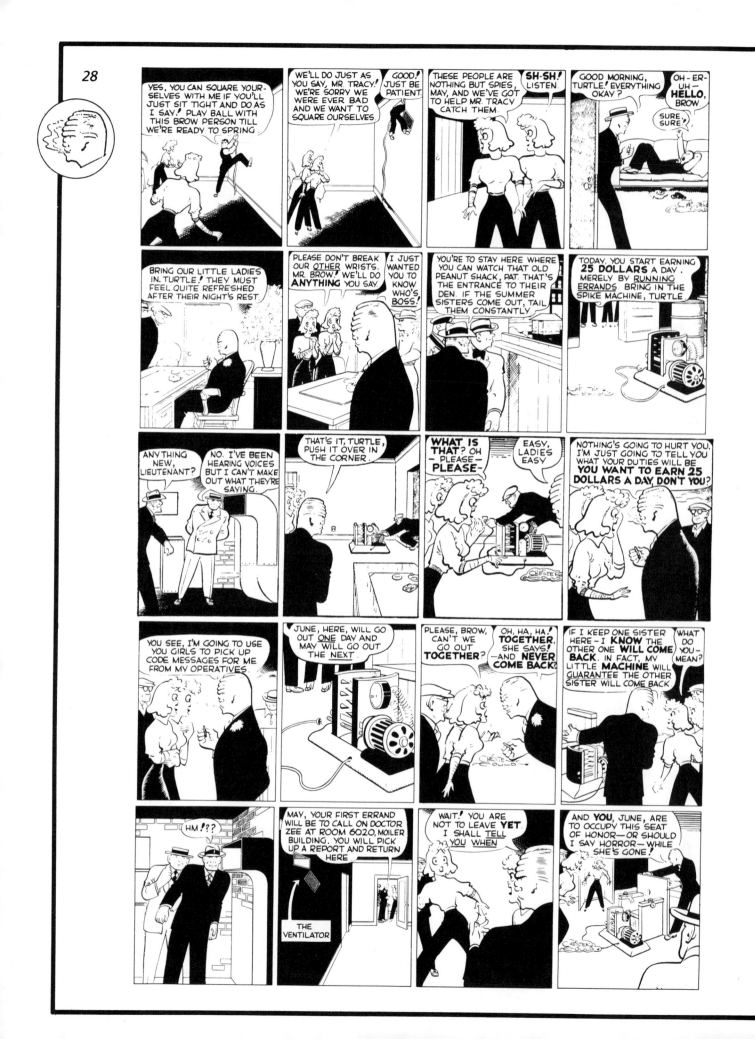

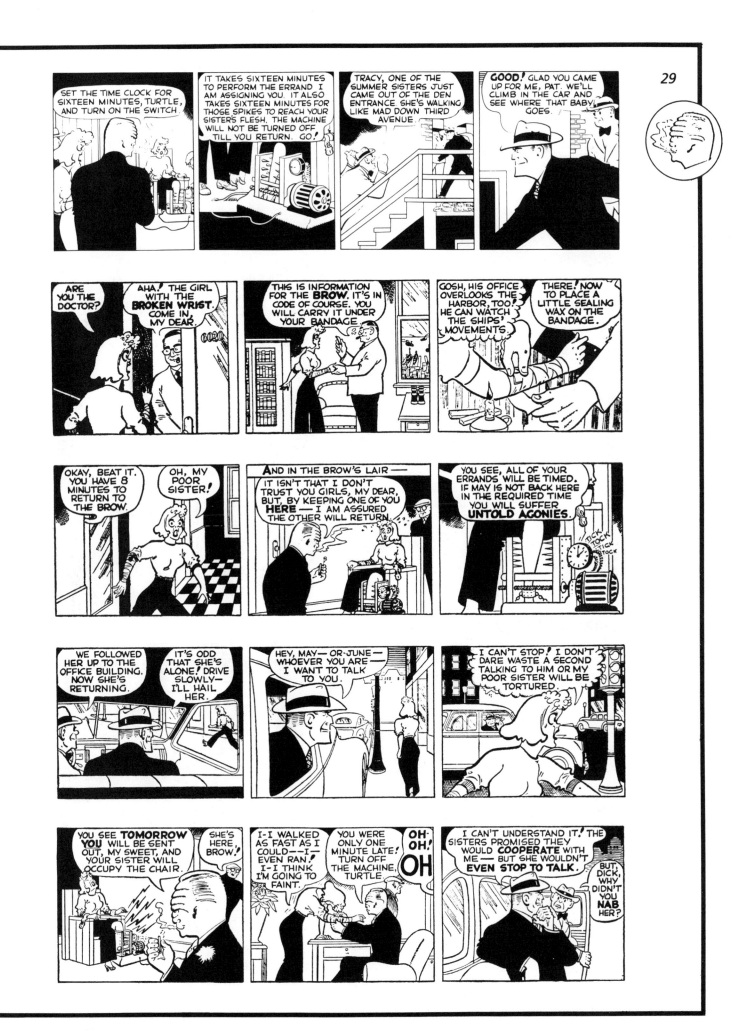

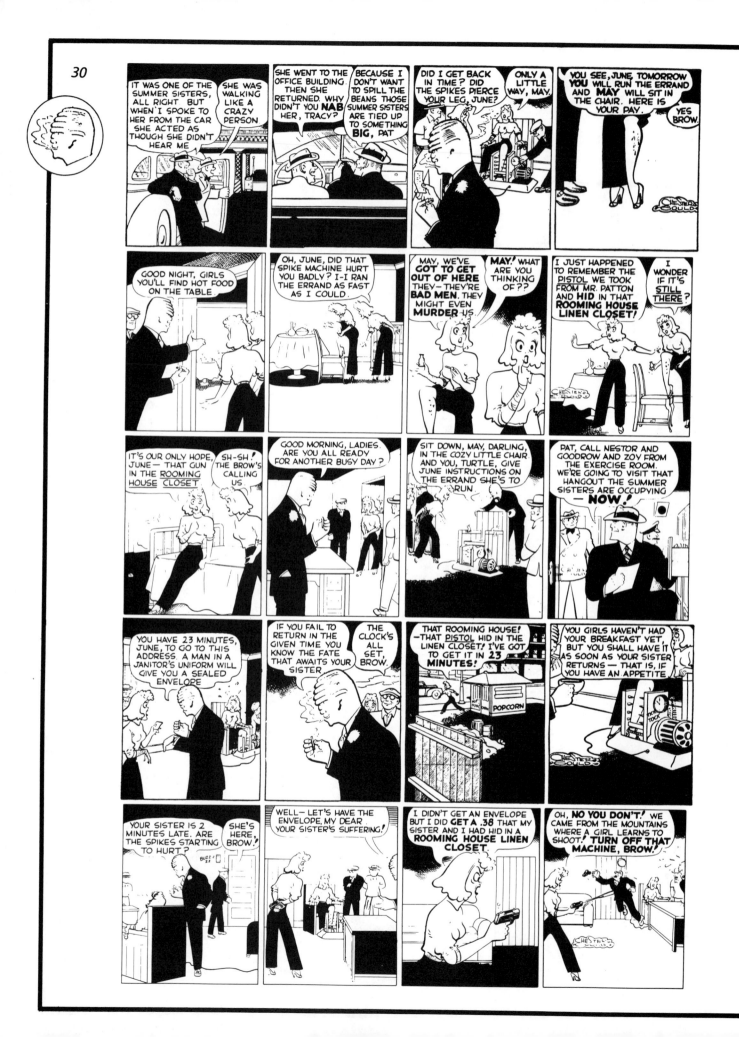

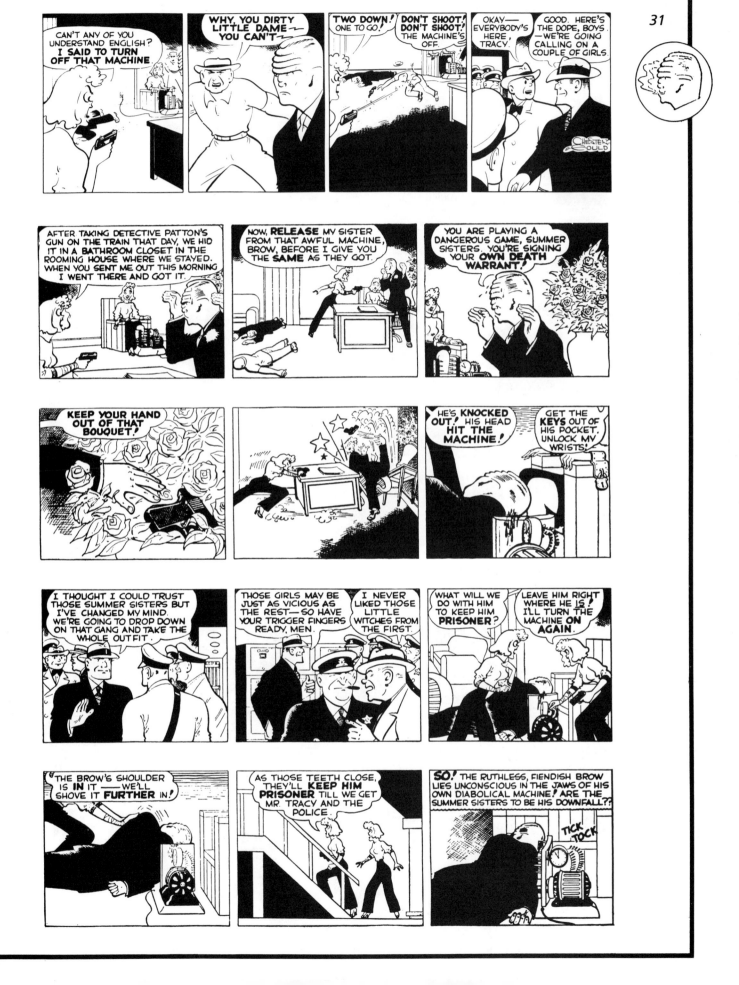

32

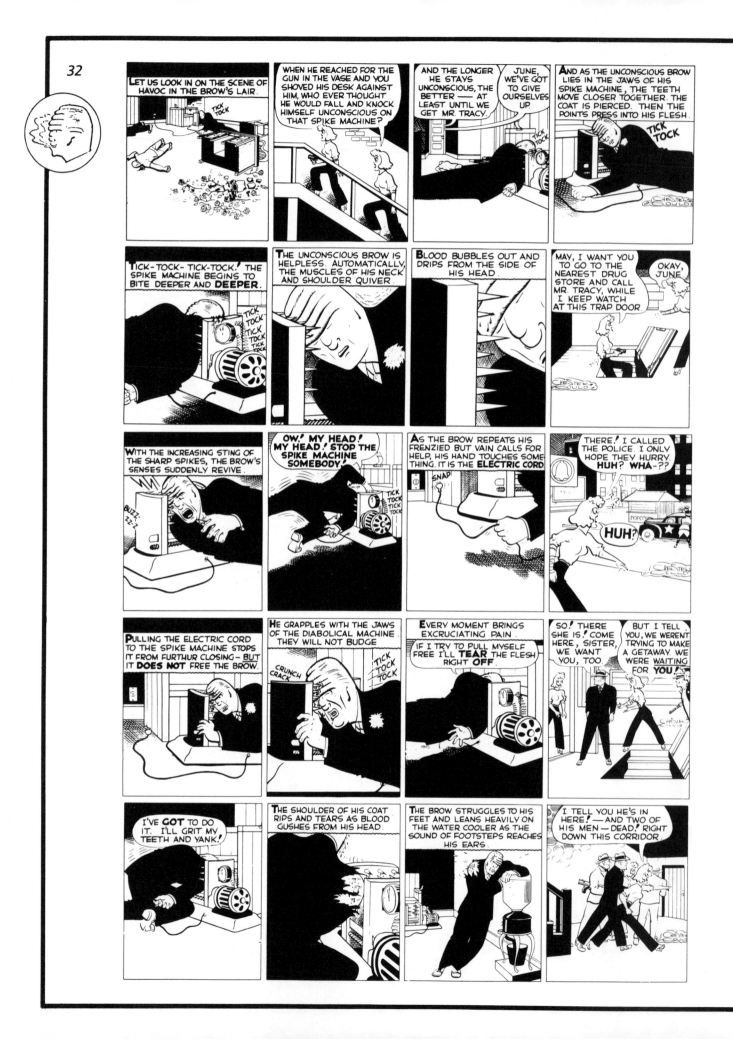

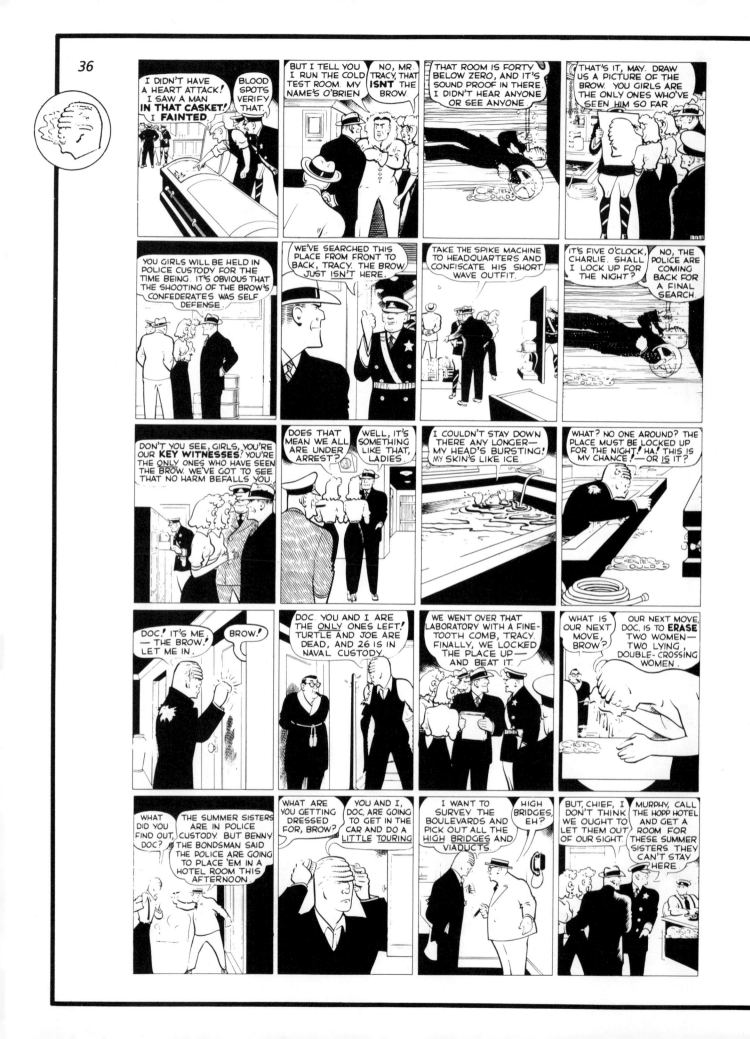

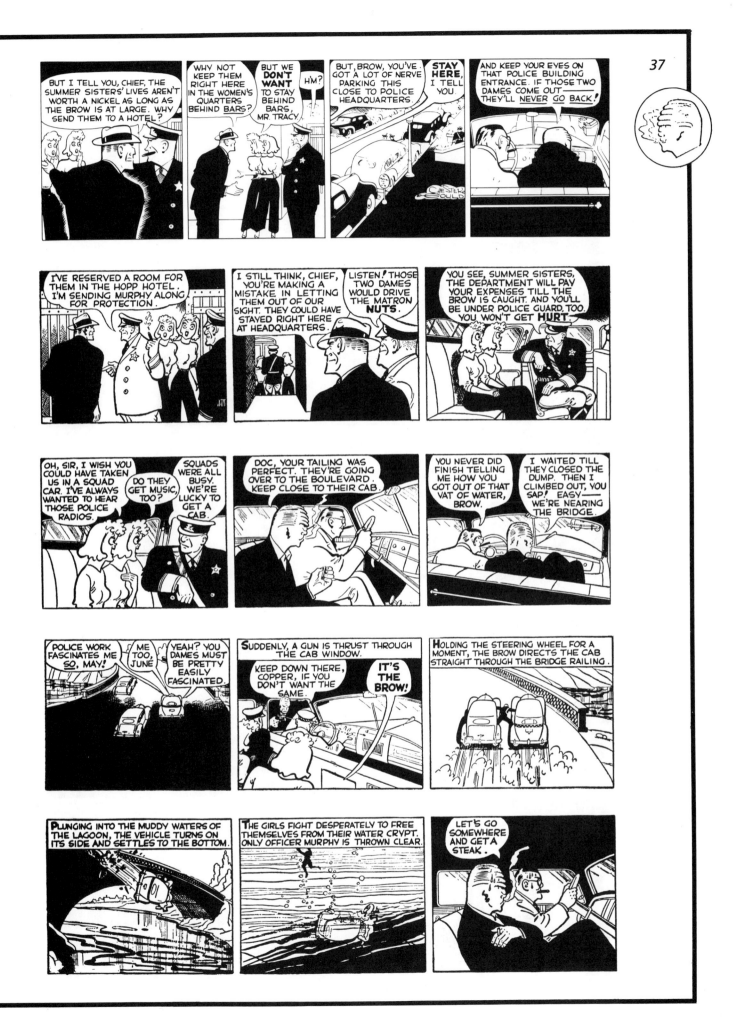

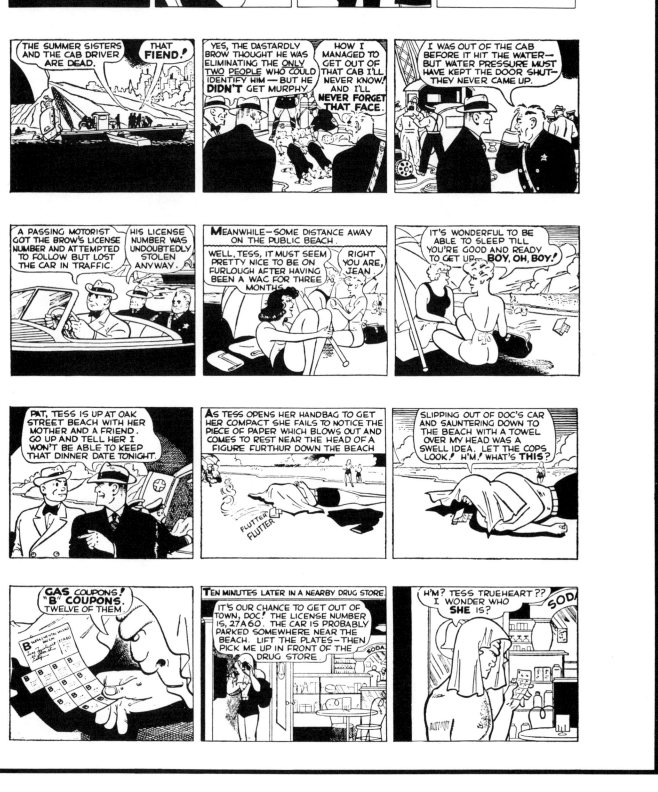

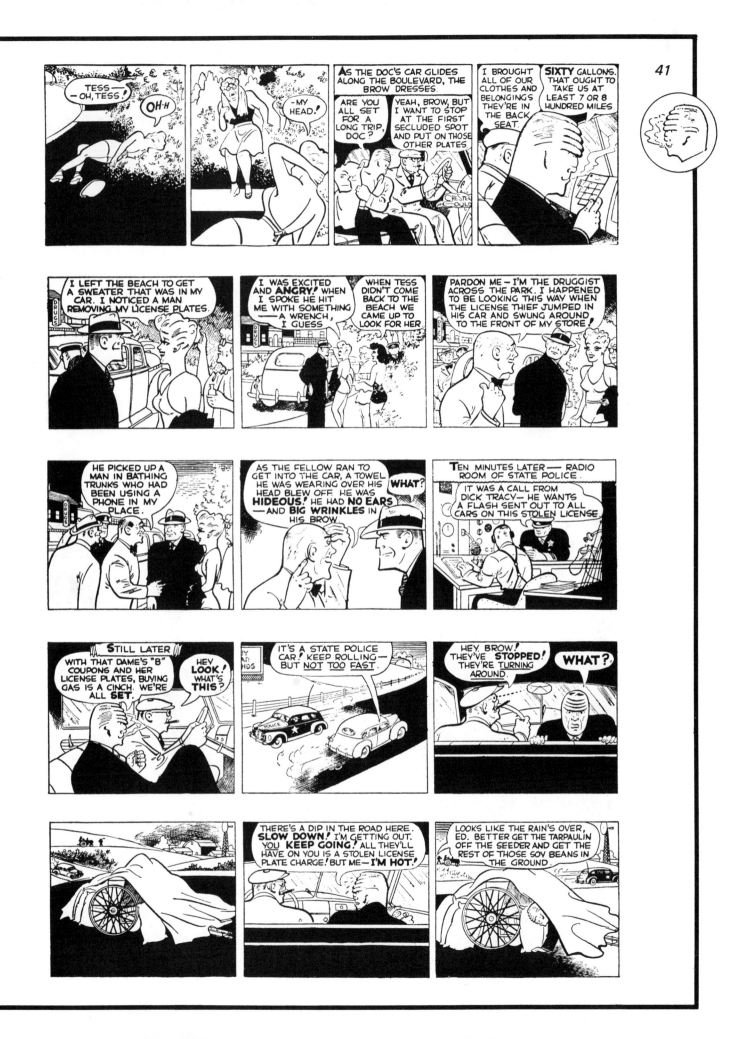

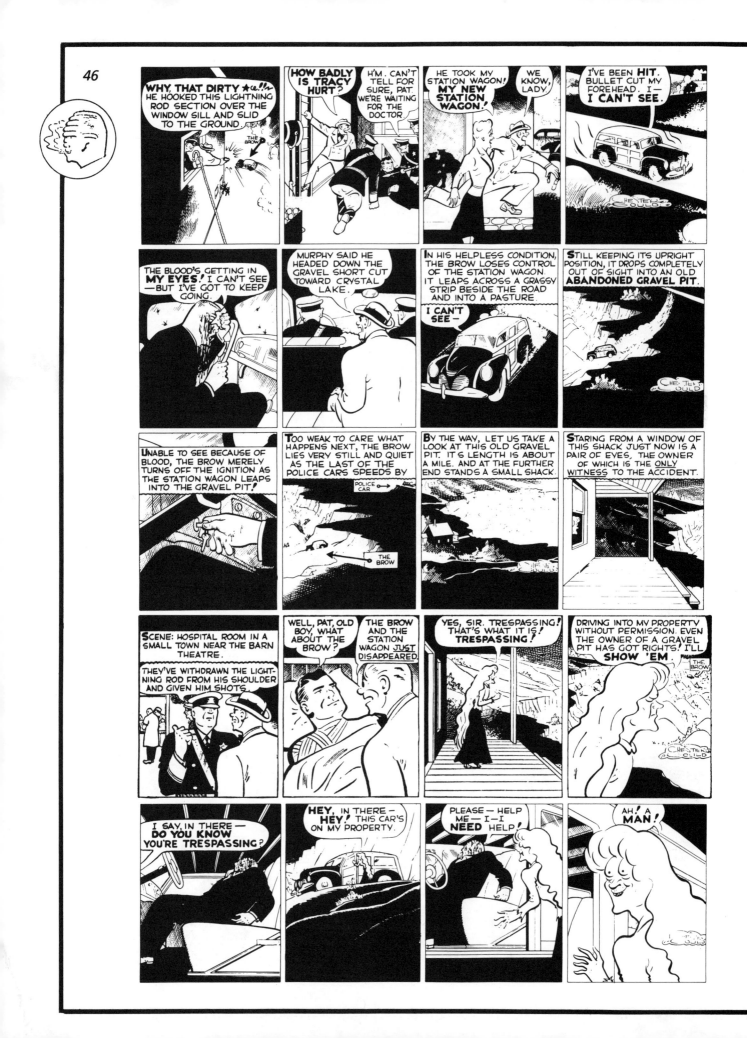

Panel 1: BUT TRACY, IT'S TRUE. THE BROW AND THE STATION WAGON **JUST DISAPPEARED!**

Panel 2: HONESTLY, I NEVER BELIEVED IN THE SUPERNATURAL **BEFORE** — BUT THIS BROW— / YOU SEE, TRACY, RIGHT AFTER WE LEFT THE THEATRE BARN—

Panel 3: EASY! I'M GETTING YOU OUT.

Panel 4: COMPANIONSHIP HAS COME TO GRAVEL GERTIE.

Panel 5: BUT IT'S **TRUE**, TRACY! WE HAD PATROLS BARRICADING ALL ROADS WITHIN 5 MINUTES AFTER THE BROW LEFT THAT BARN! HE AND THE STATION WAGON JUST **DISAPPEARED!**

Panel 6: THAT'S ODD! GRANTING THE BROW **MAY** HAVE FRIENDS LIVING IN THIS VICINITY, YOU WOULD STILL BE ABLE TO SPOT THE STATION WAGON. / WE SEARCHED EVERY FARM YARD AND GARAGE WITHIN 15 MILES.

Panel 7: THERE ARE NO SIGNS OF AN ACCIDENT! NO VISIBLE TRACKS LEAVING THE ROAD— HE **JUST** DISAPPEARED!

Panel 8: BUT LET US SEE **HOW** THE BROW DISAPPEARED. BADLY WOUNDED, HE LOSES CONTROL OF THE STATION WAGON, WHICH LEAPS INTO A GRASSY ROADSIDE SECTION AND PLUNGES STRAIGHT FORWARD INTO AN ABANDONED GRAVEL PIT.

Panel 9: IN THIS HOUR OF TRAGEDY, THE BROW'S ONLY WITNESS HAS BEEN A WITCH-LIKE CHARACTER WHOSE ABODE IS A SHACK OVERLOOKING THE SCENE.

Panel 10: NOBODY SAW YOU BUT ME. IF YOU HAD STAYED THERE YOU WOULD HAVE DIED — DIED JUST AS MY HUSBAND DIED YEARS AGO!

Panel 11: THIS USED TO BE **OUR FARM** TILL HE SOLD THE GRAVEL RIGHTS. THEY DUG UP OUR FARM— THEY LEFT A HOLE. THEN ONE DAY HE BACKED HIS CAR TOO NEAR THE EDGE.

Panel 12: YOUR HEAD IS CUT FROM THE GLASS, OR HAS IT BEEN **GRAZED BY BULLETS?** I SAW HOLES IN THE WINDSHIELD.

Panel 13: I SHALL TREAT YOUR WOUNDS! SOOT FROM A STOVE LID — THEN TO THE BASEMENT FOR SPIDER WEBS.

Panel 14: OLD FASHIONED, AM I? HA! THE CELLULOSE-LIKE SUBSTANCE IN THE SPIDER WEB CONGEALS THE BLOOD.

Panel 15: FIRST, THE WEBS — THEN THE SOOT. THE TWO BIND THE WOUND AGAINST INFECTION AND FURTHER BLEEDING.

Panel 16: YOUR NAME? **WHO** CARES?? AT **LAST**, GRAVEL GERTIE'S LONELY DAYS ARE OVER.

CAN THE BROW SURVIVE THE ANCIENT MEDICATION AT THE HANDS OF HIS WEIRD BENEFACTOR??—AND HOW LONG CAN HE ELUDE THE POLICE??

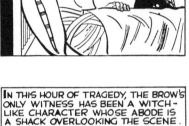

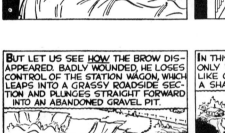

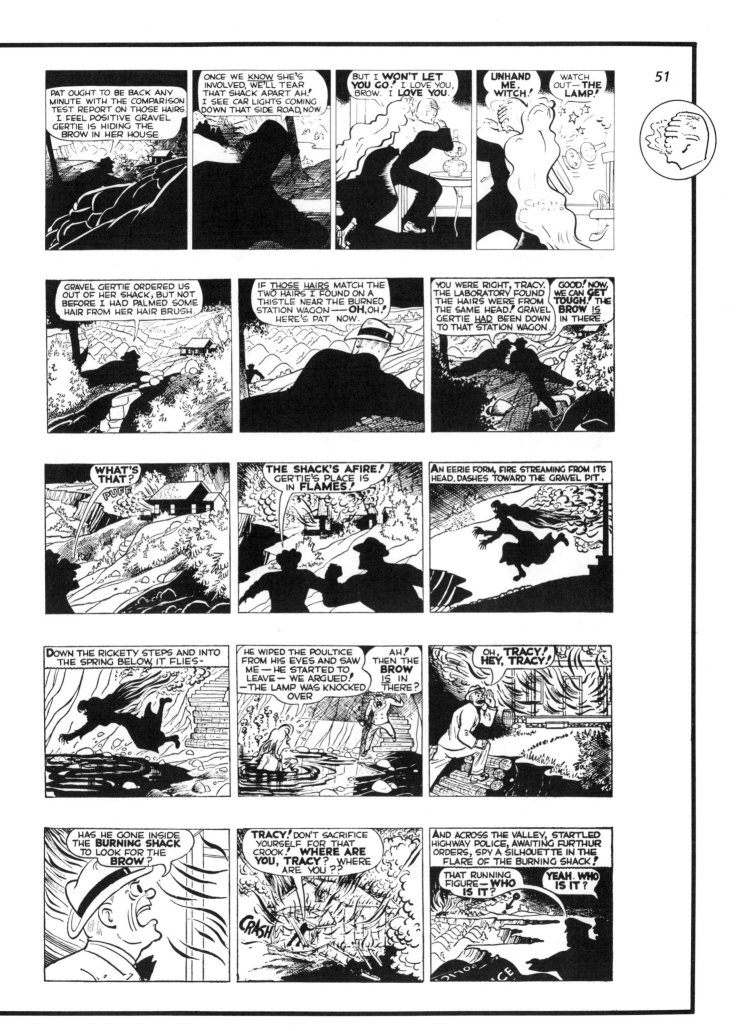

51

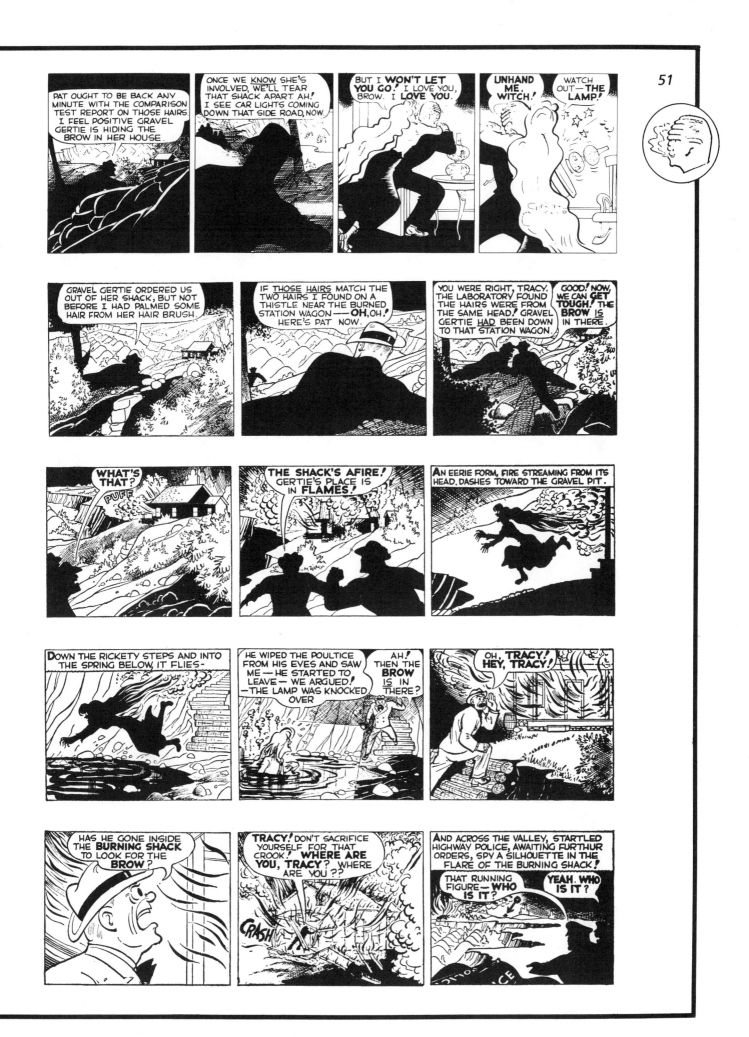

52

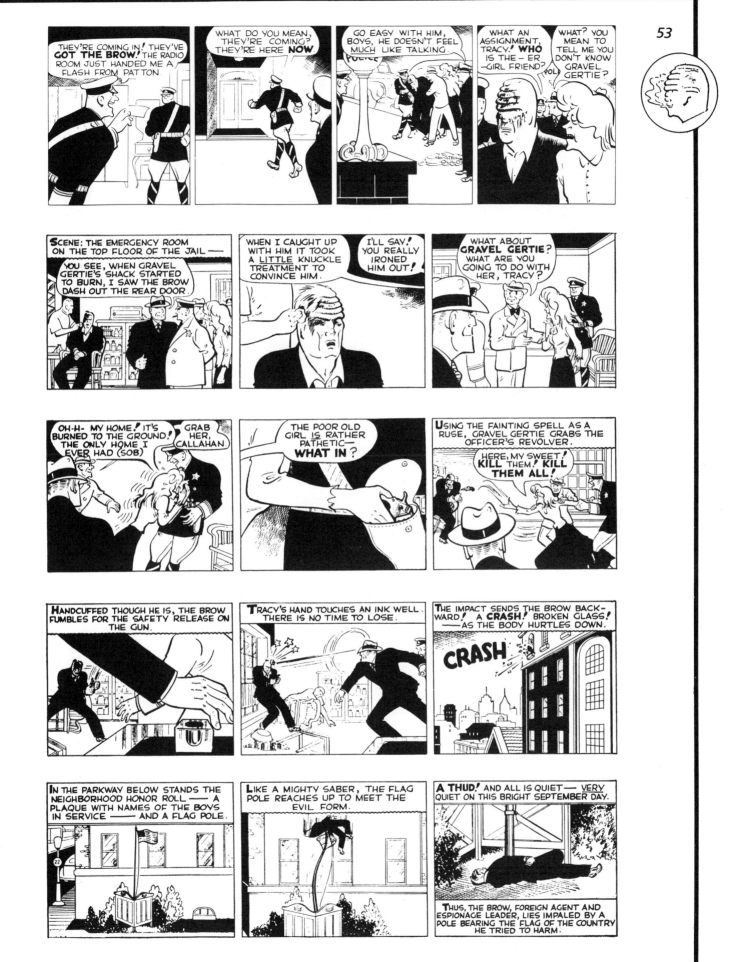

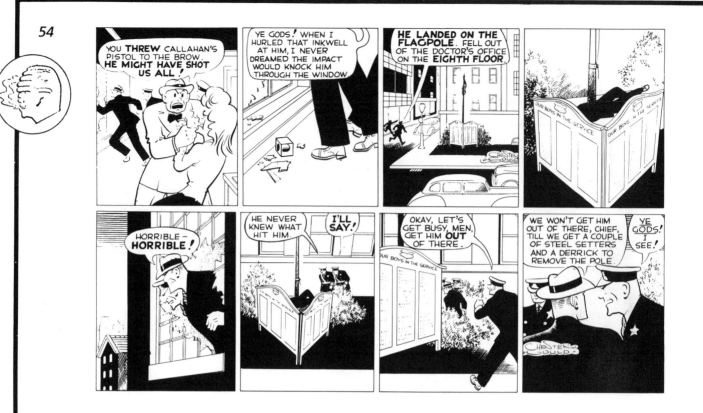

THE 1950s
CREWY LOU
by Chester Gould
5/22/51–11/4/51

The 1950s are a special era to the editors of this book. *Tracy* artist Dick Locher began assisting Chester Gould on the strip as the fifties came to a close, a dream assignment for a young cartoonist; *Tracy* writer Max Allan Collins, as a young boy, discovered the strip in the early 1950s and has been fascinated with fictional detectives and crime ever since.

If the 1940s represent the pinnacle of *Tracy*'s commercial success, and the moment when Gould "put it together" creatively, the early 1950s represent Gould at his mature best.

This 1951 continuity, dubbed "The Case of the Fiendish Photographers" in the Harvey Comics serialization coeditor Collins followed circa 1954, may be Gould's masterpiece. A few months before the beginning of this continuity, Gould began drawing his originals smaller, reflecting the smaller size the strip was printed in in most newspapers (paper shortages during the war opened the door to editors shrinking the publication size of comics). Now somewhat limited visually, Gould poured on the steam where the stories themselves were concerned. Certainly this story—the first complete continuity of the shrunken-art period—demonstrates Gould flexing his

every muscle as a writer.

The soap opera elements of the thirties are represented by the happy home life of the Tracys with their new daughter, Bonnie Braids, at the outset, and by the dramatic and moving disappearance of the child as the story progresses.

The depiction of crime—with small-time con-men/thieves Crewy Lou and Sphinx coming up against a Big Boy-like underworld kingpin—is at once reminiscent of Gould's thirties era outlaws and gangsters, yet more realistic, right out of W. R. Burnett or Dashiell Hammett, but updated. The "King" is definitely a post-war, executive-style organized crime figure we've not met before in *Dick Tracy*.

At the same time, we have the trademark violent action, with bullets flying, villains meeting grisly deaths; a villainess leading Tracy on an extended perilous chase; Tracy himself portrayed as an astute detective *and* a fast-shooting lawman *and* a tortured father.

And we have a charismatic adversary in Crewy Lou, a crafty three-dimensional human being who holds our attention and even, oddly, our sympathy.

59

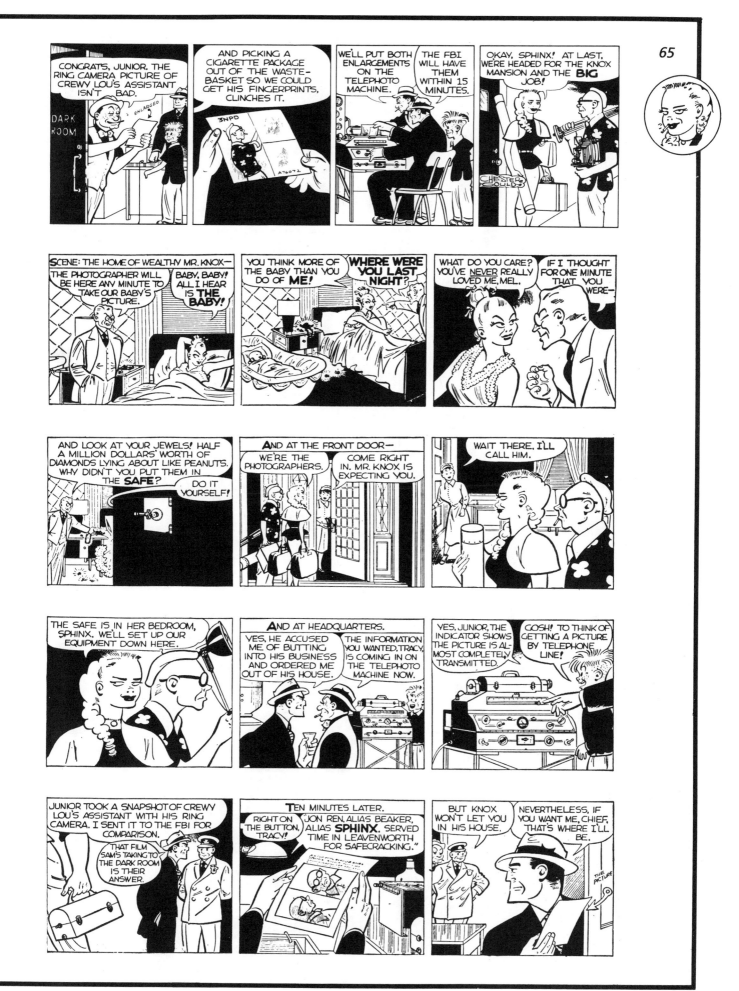

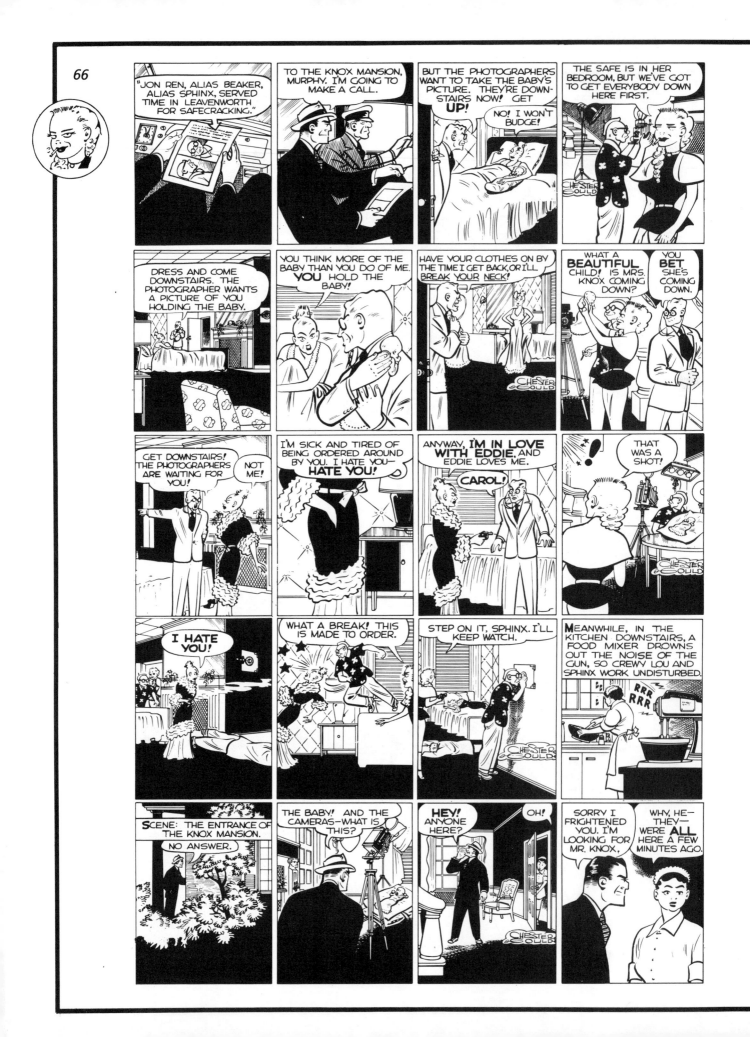

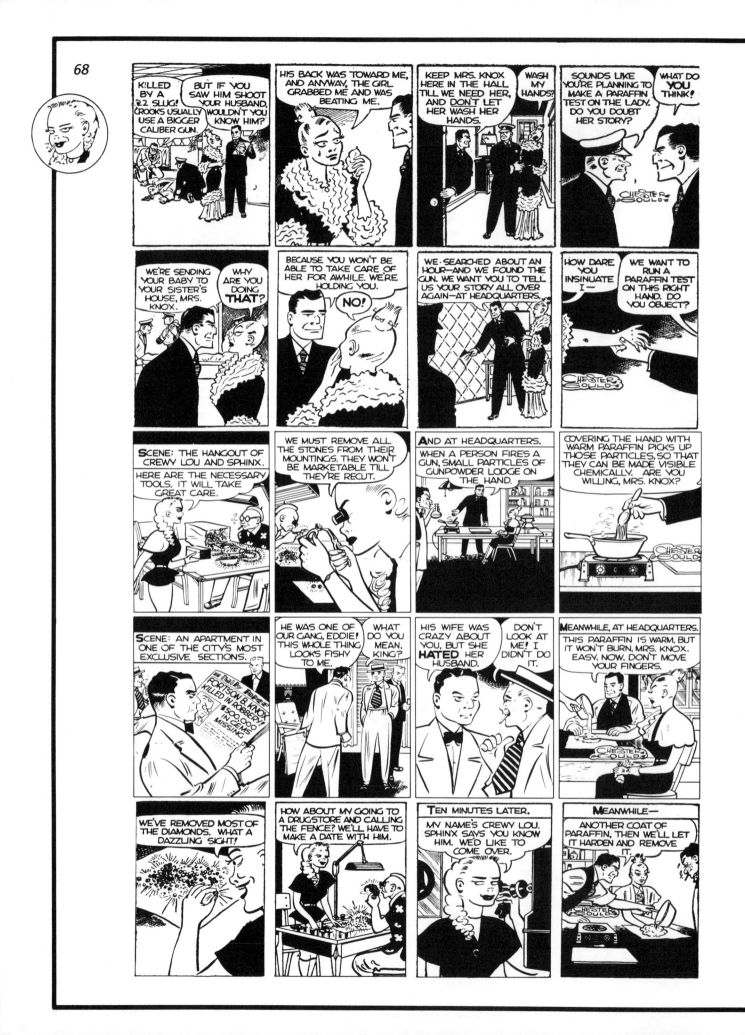

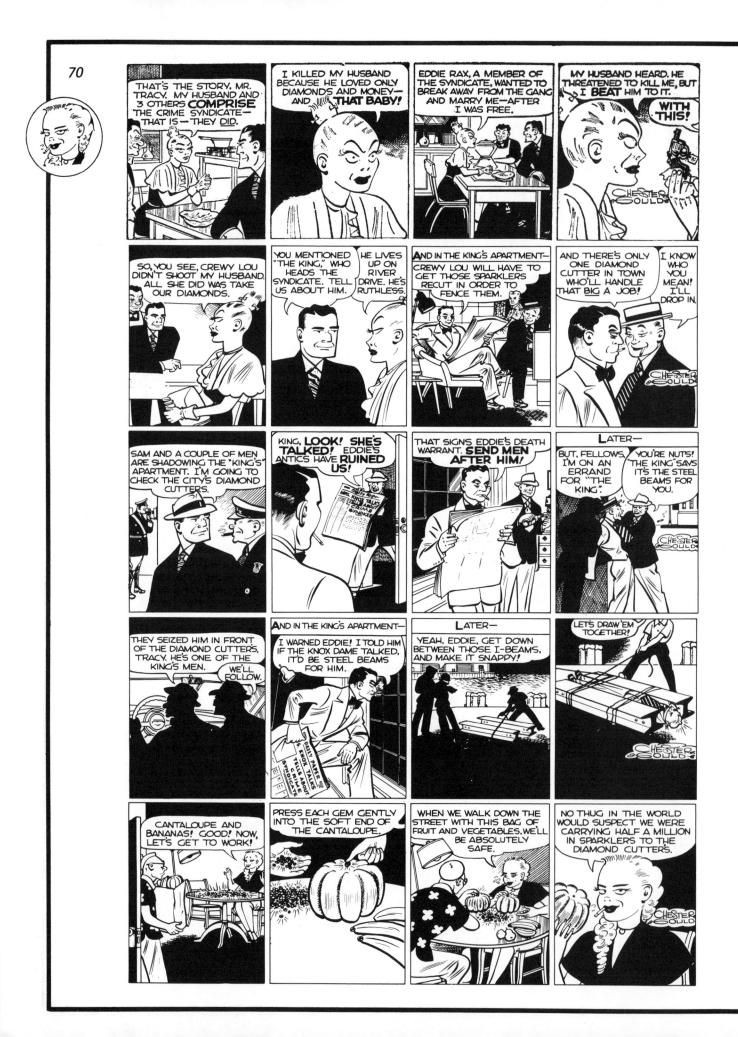

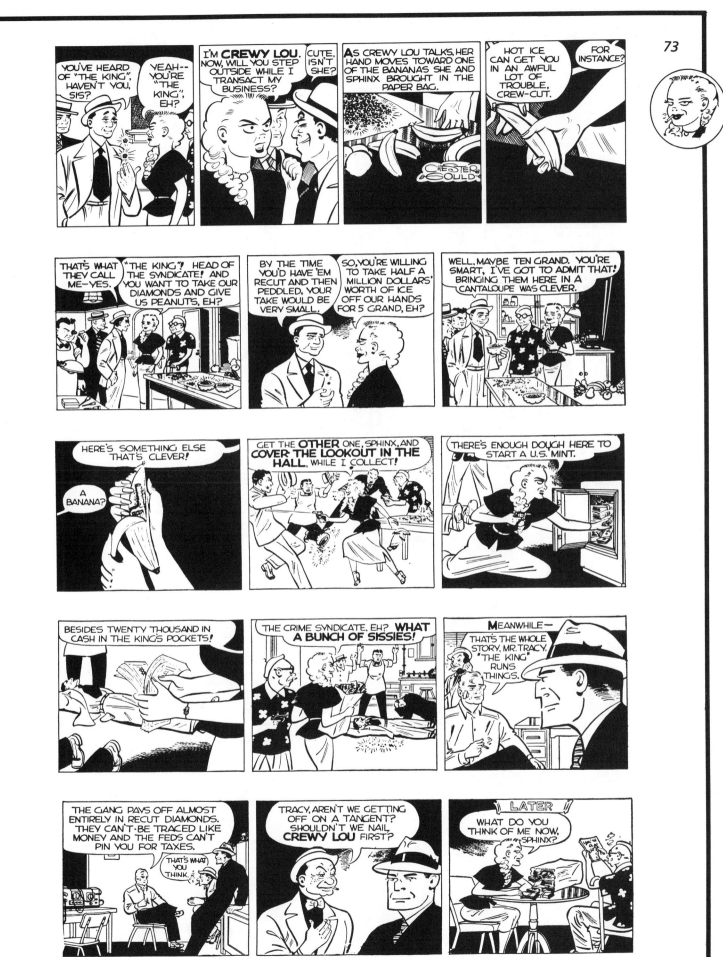

74

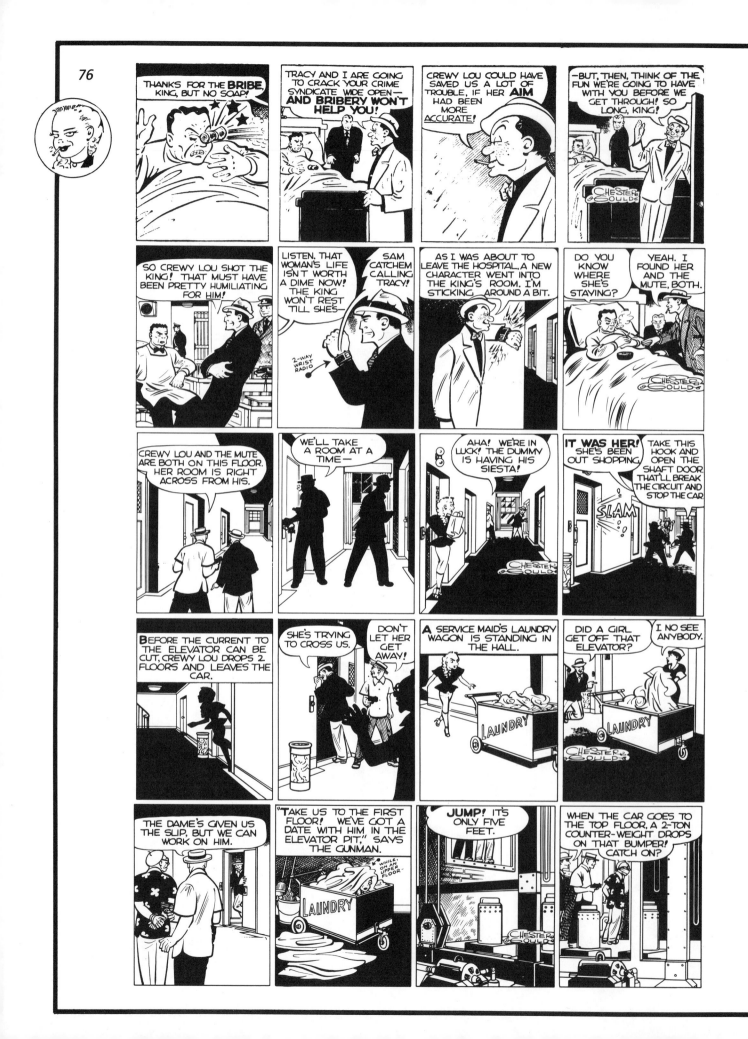

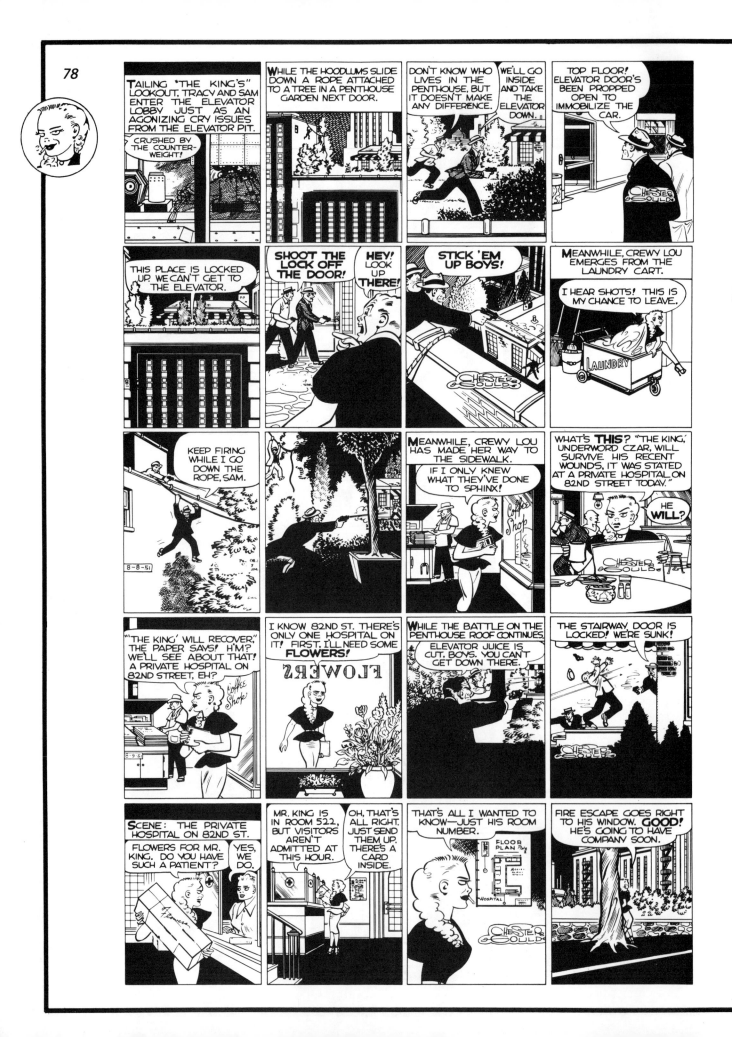

78

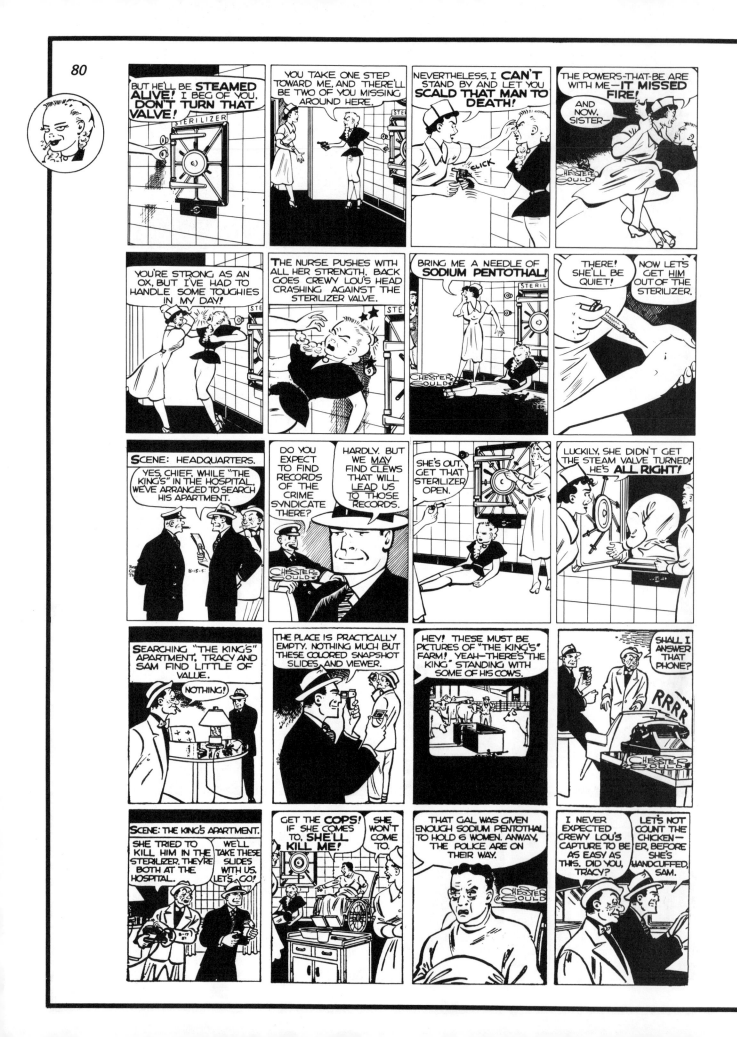

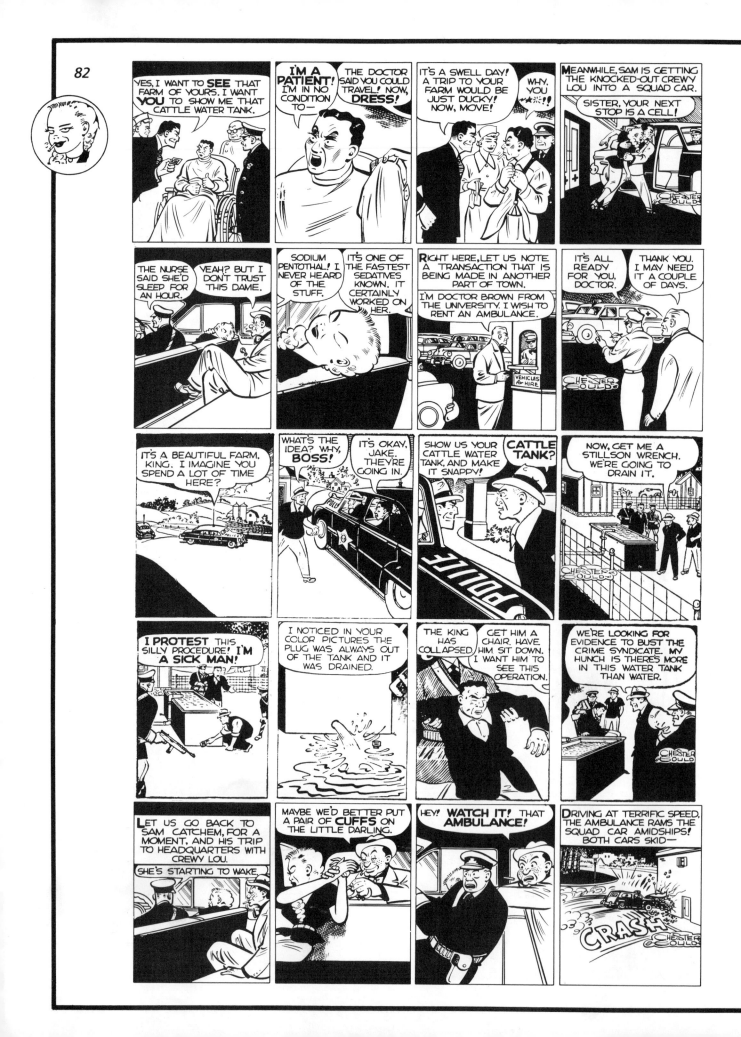

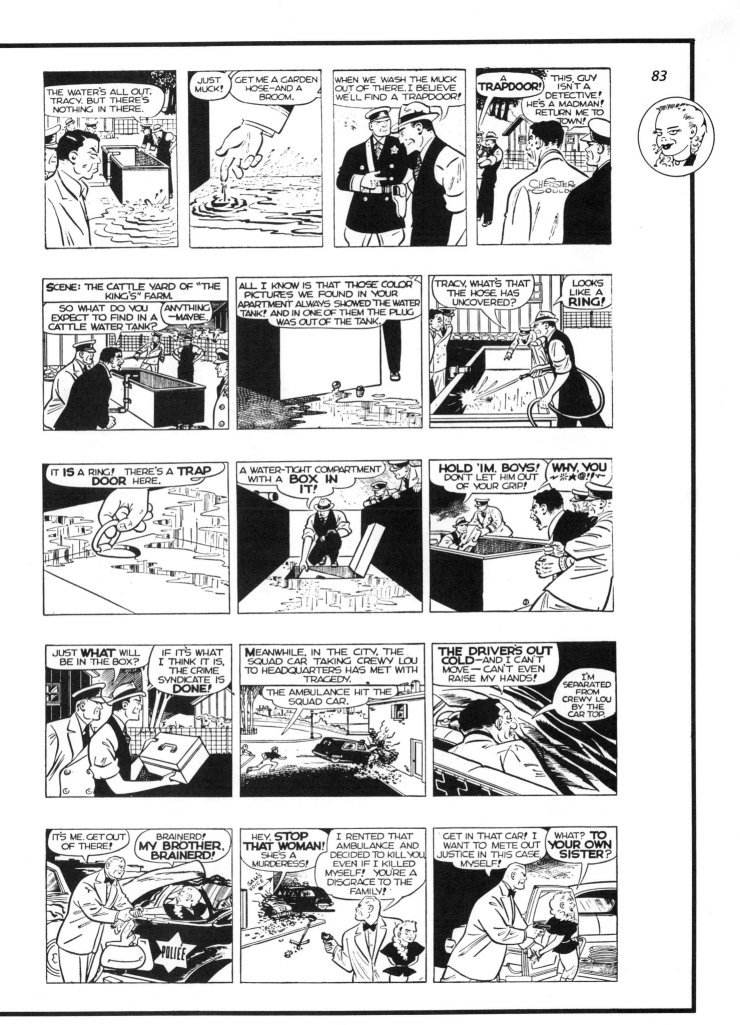

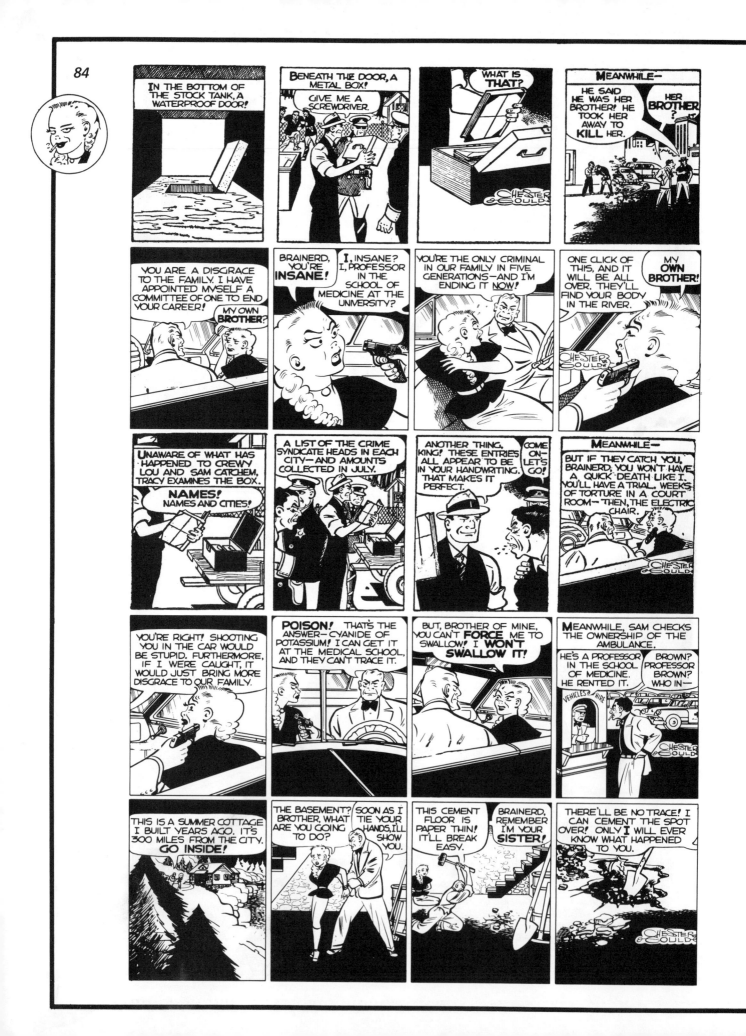

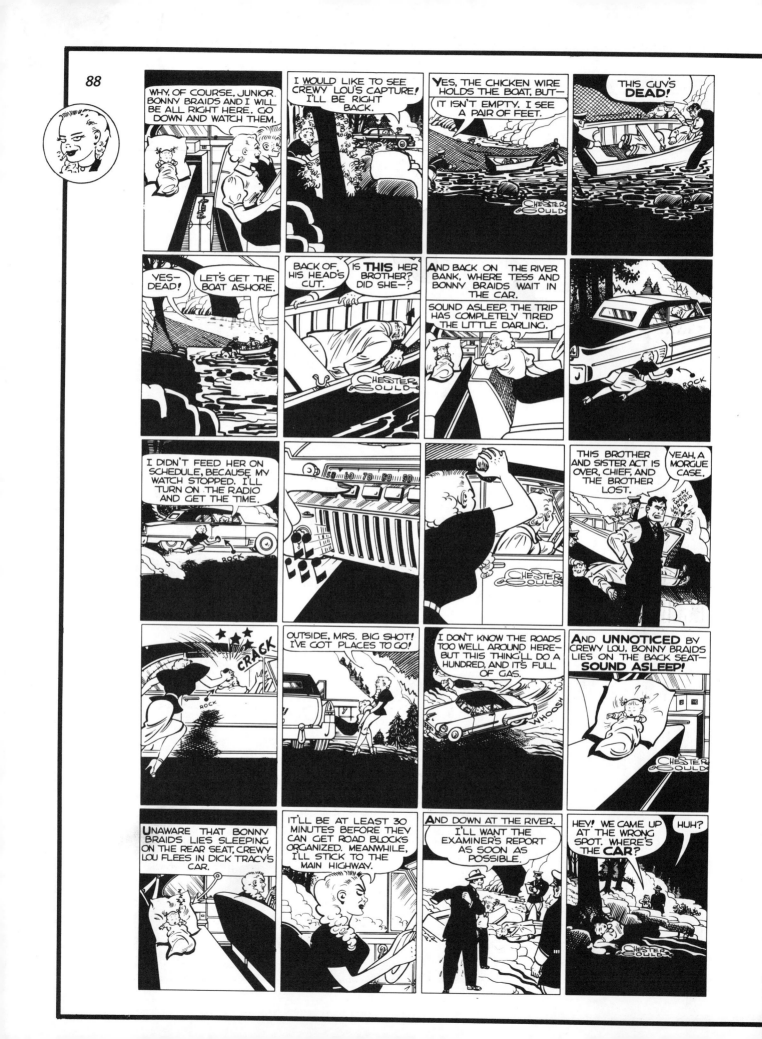

NO WORD ON THE BABY. SEARCHING PARTIES ARE BEING ORGANIZED.

AT HEADQUARTERS. TRACY AND SAM ARE AT DIET SMITH'S AIRPORT NOW. THEY'RE REFUELING THE HELICOPTER.

AND AT DIET SMITH'S— I'M TURNING IT OVER TO THE POLICE DEPARTMENT TO USE TILL THE CHILD IS FOUND. MY PILOT WILL FLY YOU.

AND CREWY LOU DRIVES ON— I MUST BE 15 MILES BACK IN THE MOUNTAINS. NOBODY WOULD BELIEVE A CAR COULD MAKE IT. THEY'LL NEVER FIND ME!

91

NO WORD— NO WORD?

NO WORD—

NO WORD— NO WORD! OH, BONNY BRAIDS, MY BABY! WHAT HAVE THEY DONE WITH YOU?

MRS. TRACY—PLEASE! TRY TO CONTROL YOURSELF. THE TELEPHONE.

I'M AT DIET SMITH'S FACTORY. HE'S LENDING THE POLICE DEPARTMENT HIS HELICOPTER. WE'RE TAKING OFF IN TEN MINUTES.

THERE'S NO TRACE OF THE CAR! OUR ROAD BLOCKS HAVE BEEN PERFECT, BUT THE CAR HAS VANISHED! GET THE MAPS, SAM.

VANISHED? WELL, ALMOST! THE PANICKY, FEAR-CRAZED CREWY LOU, BEHIND THE WHEEL OF TRACY'S CAR, IS TRAVELING A MOUNTAIN PATH.

ROCKS, NARROW PASSES, FALLEN TREES! NO AUTOMOBILE EVER TOOK SUCH PUNISHMENT.

RACING MOTOR! BURNING RUBBER! BENT FENDERS! THEY'LL BE DAYS FINDING ME! MEANWHILE, I'LL THINK OF SOMETHING!

AS FOR YOU—YOUR BEING ALONG WAS AN ACCIDENT. I'M NOT RESPONSIBLE!

"WHEN I ABANDON THIS CRATE, YOU'LL BE EXCESS BAGGAGE—YOU'LL BE LEFT RIGHT HERE."

IT'S HER FEEDING TIME AGAIN! SHE'S MISSED THREE OF HER FEEDINGS— OH, MY BABY! NOW, MRS. TRACY.

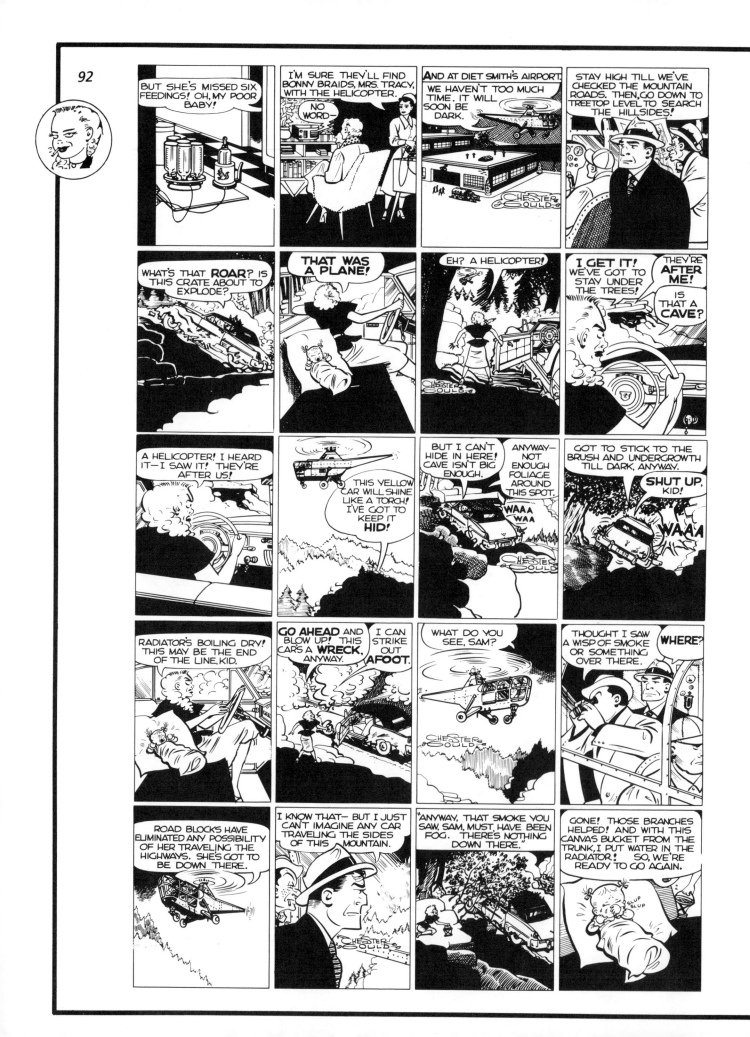

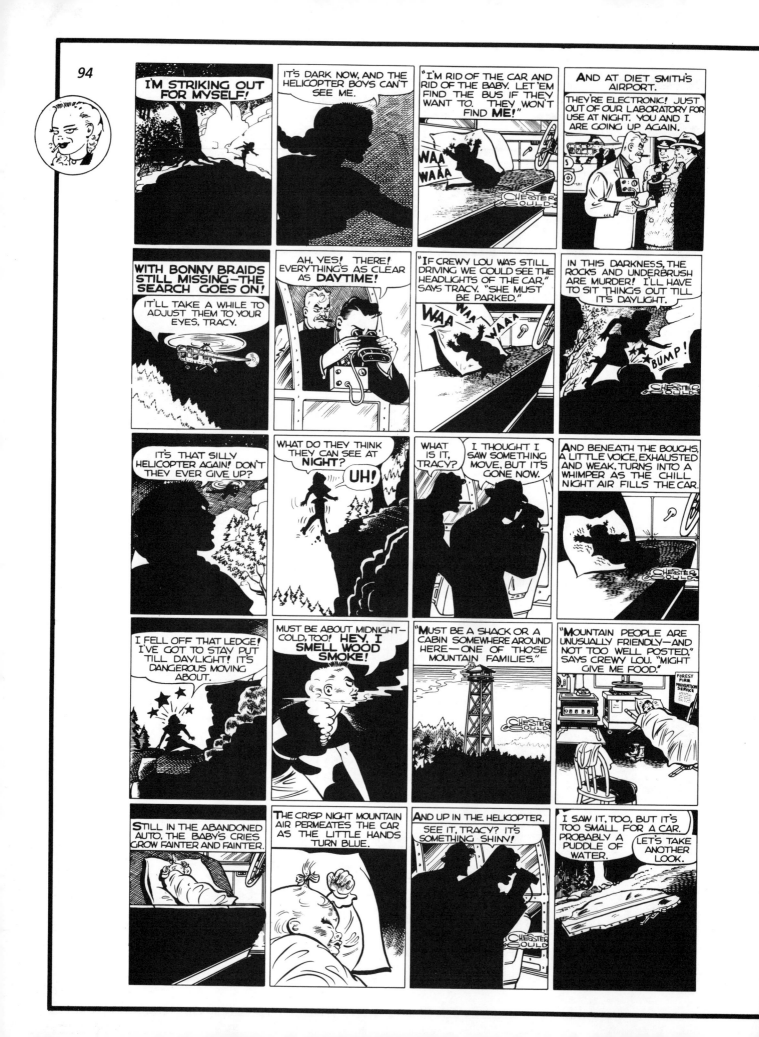

96

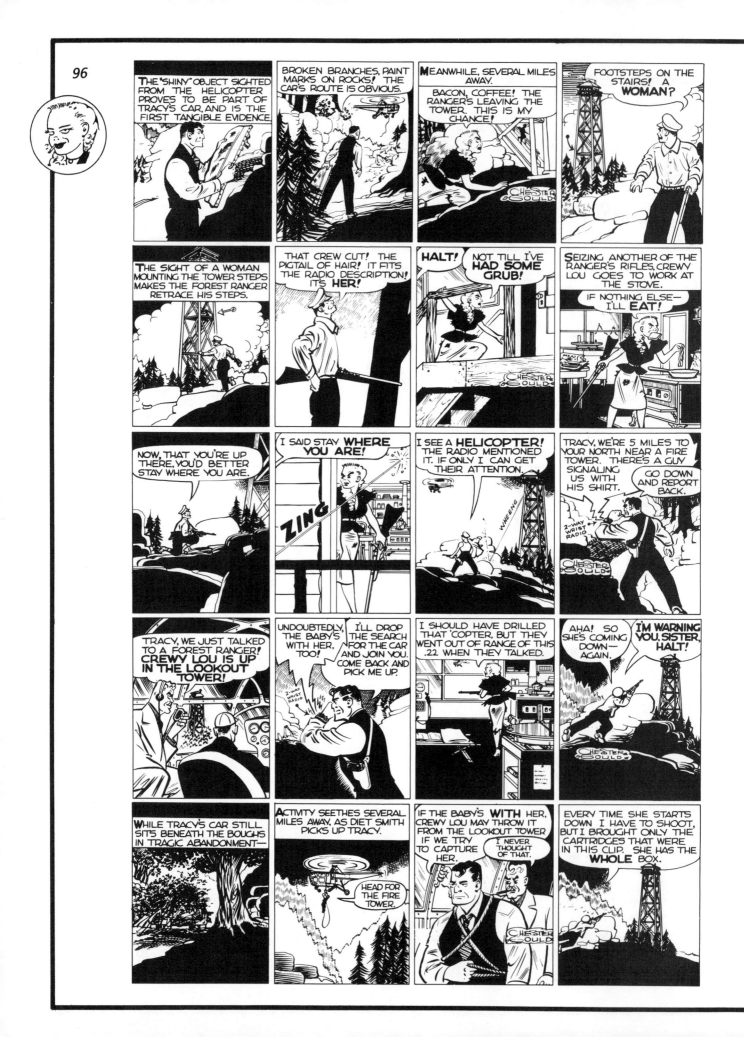

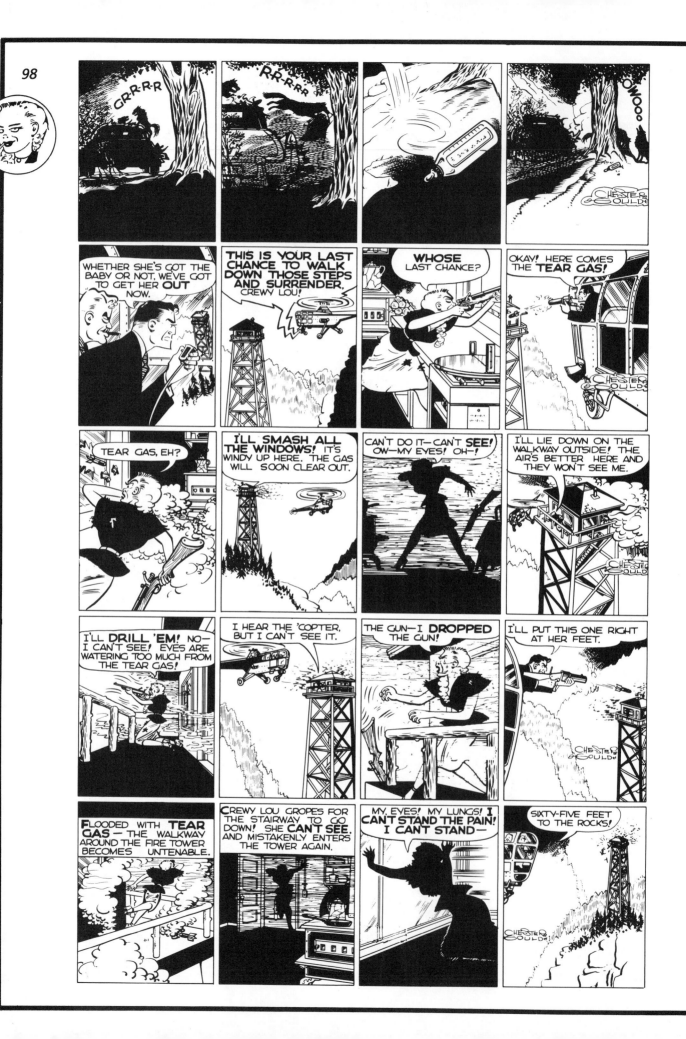

98

MODEL
by Chester Gould
1/23/52–3/27/52

Because the 1950s are such a strong and under-reprinted period of Gould's work, and because these years have a special meaning to the editors of this volume, we have chosen to include a second fifties continuity.

The uncharacteristically brief "Model" story harks back slightly to the earlier soap-opera period of *Dick Tracy*'s formative thirties. Significantly, in those years, Tracy's adoptive son Junior, an urchin who wanted to be a detective like his father, was a major character. By the early fifties, this male Orphan Annie was outdated, and Gould decided to bring Junior "of age." Junior, with his wacky hacked-off haircut, is suddenly a teenager, and in meeting the sweet, lovely Model Jones at a skating rink, has his first romance.

This tender story reveals that the hard-boiled, right-wing Gould was not unaffected by certain social concerns of the times. Model's brother Larry is a j.d. who loots parking meters, and their parents are alcoholics. Gould places the responsibility for Larry's actions clearly at his parents' feet.

While this love story may seem a departure for Gould, he does not cut back on the violence or the action; a rooftop chase, near the end of the story, shows the detective in fine heroic form. Tracy's world is a precarious one, where anything can happen, and even the most sympathetic of creatures can fall prey to crime.

And if Gould, during this period, was putting his emphasis on the story, in response to the shrinking size his work (and the work of his fellow cartoonists) was suffering at the hands of newspaper editors, he does not shirk his artistic responsibilities. Note the moving sequence when Junior is rebuffed by his girl; the bleak, expressionistic winter landscape Junior slouch-shoulderedly moves through is hauntingly evocative of the boy's mental state. Some of the best writing in comics is done through silent panels, as witness the sequences in which a despondent Model slumps in her seat on the bus while in the adjacent panel Junior watches dejectedly as the bus recedes in the distance.

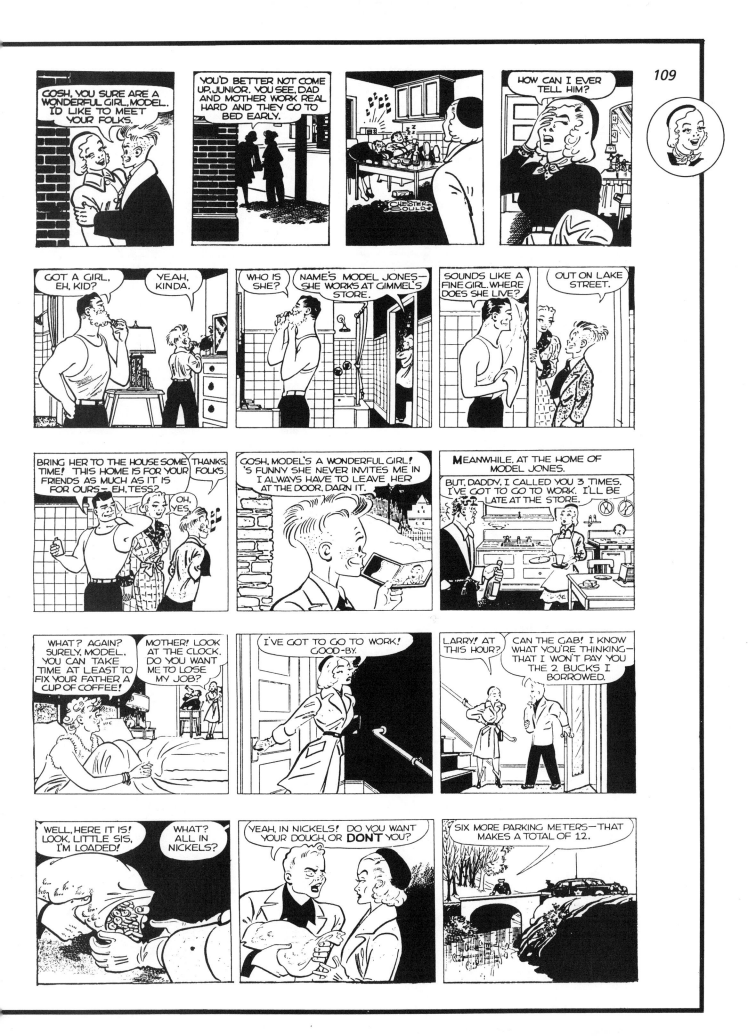

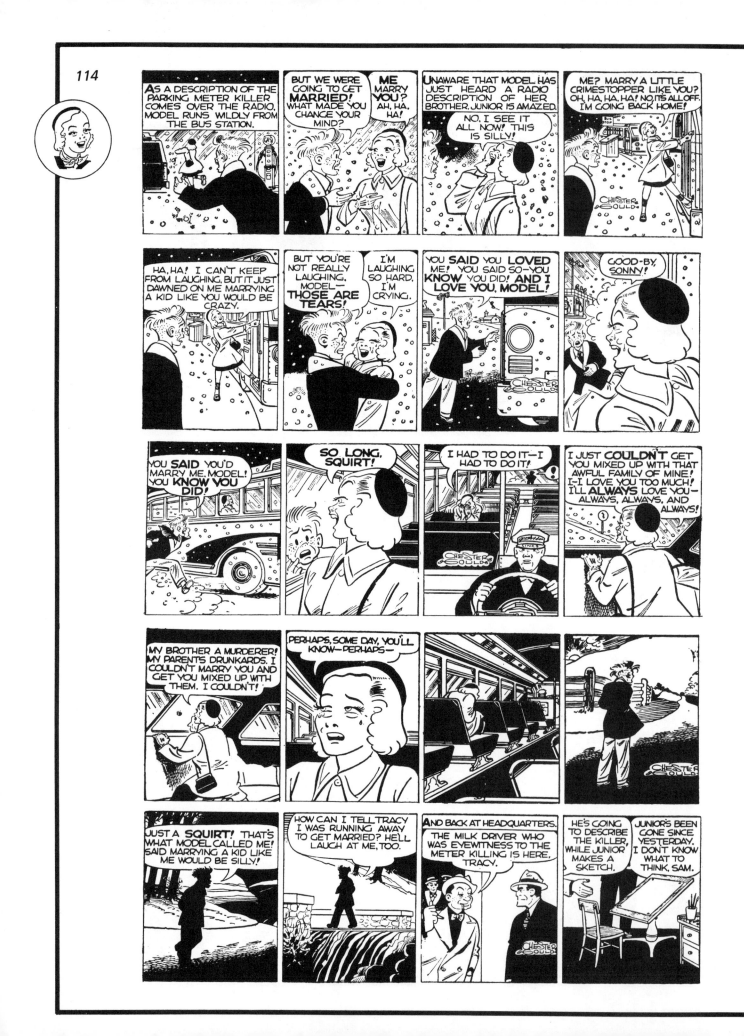

115

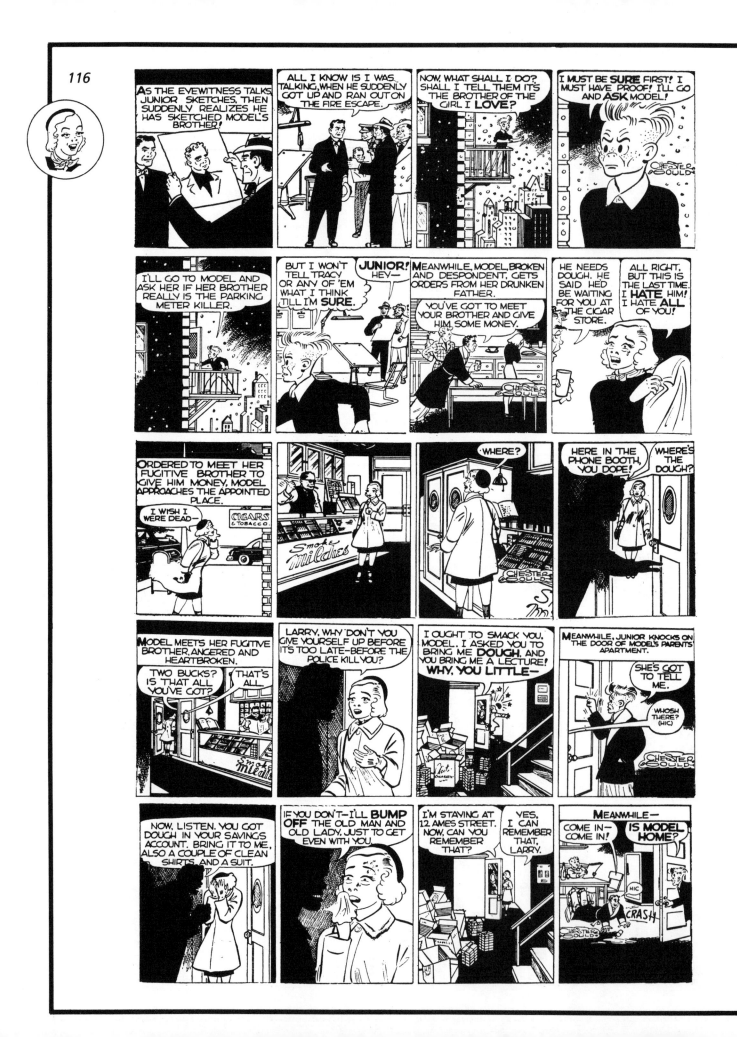

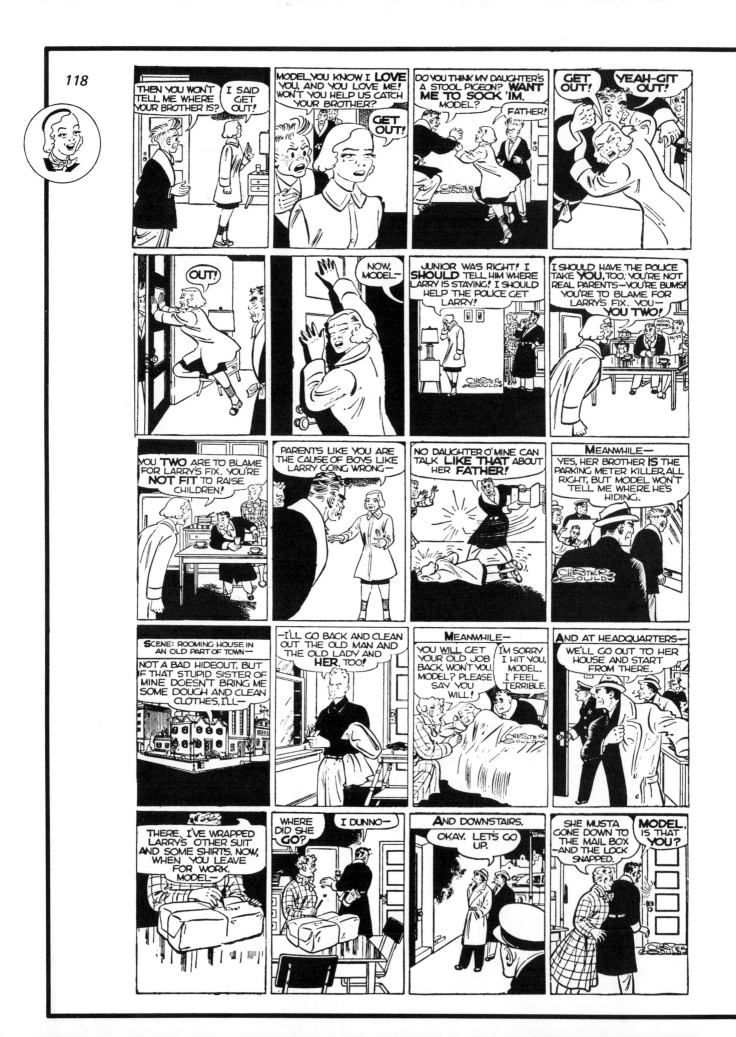

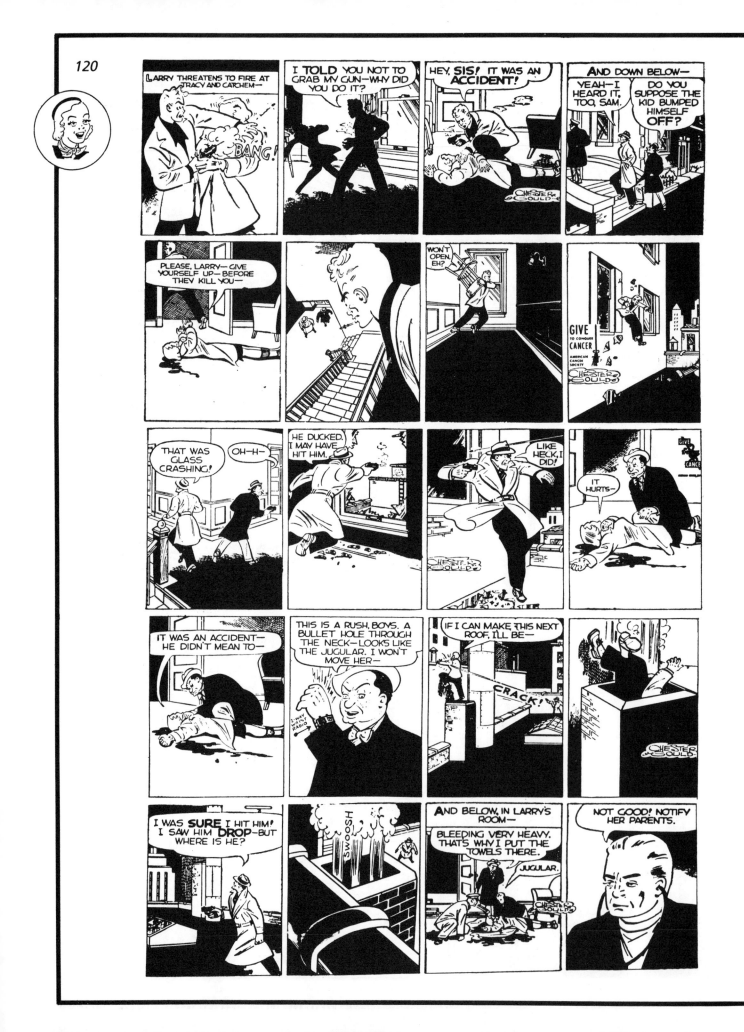

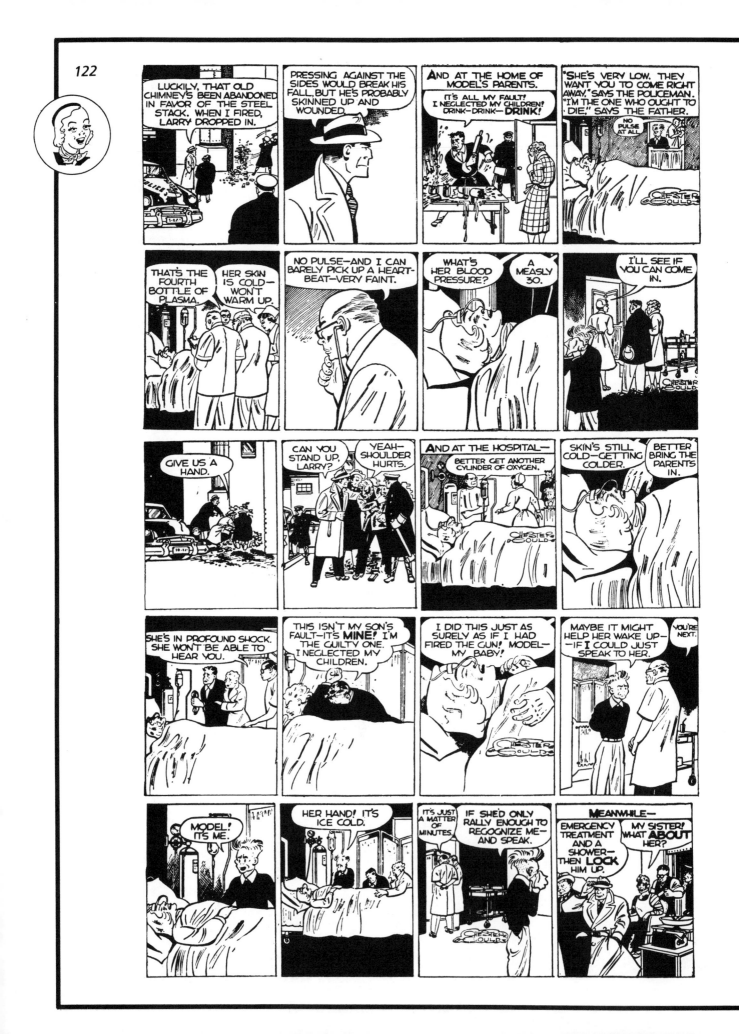

124

THE 1960s
SPOTS
by Chester Gould
8/3/60–11/30/60

The 1960s were by no one's yardstick the glory years for Chester Gould's *Dick Tracy*. Gould's diatribes against hippies and his "Law and Order First" campaign made the once cutting-edge strip seem to some readers crankily, creakily Establishment-oriented. (Ironically, many counterculture "underground" cartoonists—including Art Spiegelman, Kim Deitch, Gilbert Shelton, and Robert Crumb, who visited Gould's Tribune Tower office in the late sixties—continued to extol the virtues of *Tracy*'s creator, both for his storytelling and his graphic mastery.)

Gould's decision to take Tracy to the moon pleased few of his fans, though Chet himself loved these sequences. Marrying Junior Tracy off to the exotic Moon Maid seemed, to some of the faithful, a mistake of major proportions: In the late forties and the fifties, Gould had clearly set events in motion so that Junior would one day marry Sparkle Plenty (whom Moon Maid resembled in some regards). And outfitting Tracy and crew in flying magnetic moon buckets violated Gould's stated intention to keep Tracy only one simple remove away from reality. Taking Tracy into outer space, and giving him science fiction gadgetry, went well beyond the Two-Way Wrist Radio, satellite television hookups, and openheart surgery, to name a few of Gould's one-step-ahead-of-the-times visions.

In fact, Tracy didn't beat Neil Armstrong to the moon by *that* many years, did he?

Nonetheless, the moon sequences represent Gould's wonderful imagination at its least disciplined. Editors and readers were as uncomfortable with Tracy in a Space Coupe as they'd have been with Buck Rogers or Flash Gordon in a squad car.

Also, Gould's wonderfully tight storylines of the 1940s, and especially of the early 1950s, had begun to meander. Gould did not plot ahead, and felt if he didn't know what was going to happen next, neither would the reader; this philosophy served him well for decades. And the stories of the 1960s remained very effective, taken in daily doses; but when read in one sitting, they are less successful.

The strengths of the 1960s, in fact, are not in the area of story; where the sixties shine is in the artwork. These years might be described as Gould's pop-art period; his dramatic use of striking black-and-white composition hit its peak around 1968. (The assistants during this period were the two artists who would later, individually, take over the *Tracy* art chores: coeditor Dick Locher and Rick Fletcher.) Particularly in his depiction of weather and terrain, Gould was (as Richard Marschall has described him) a "wildly successful" Expressionist. The strip had never looked better, particularly the dynamic, stunningly designed Sunday pages. This is the period that influenced Warhol, Lichenstein, and other purveyors of pop art.

We have chosen a sequence that merges some of these pop-art tendencies with the last, pre-moon gasp of Gould's better writing. Spots is a terrific villain, who somewhat resembles the earlier thirties fiend the Blank, and the doggerel-spouting poet Ogden represents Gould's zany humor at its most offbeat. And the demise of Spots is particularly memorable.

Coeditor Locher was Gould's assistant at the time of this continuity; he and Gould also collaborated on an extensive sequence in 1958, which resulted in the strip's first National Cartoonists Society Reuben award.

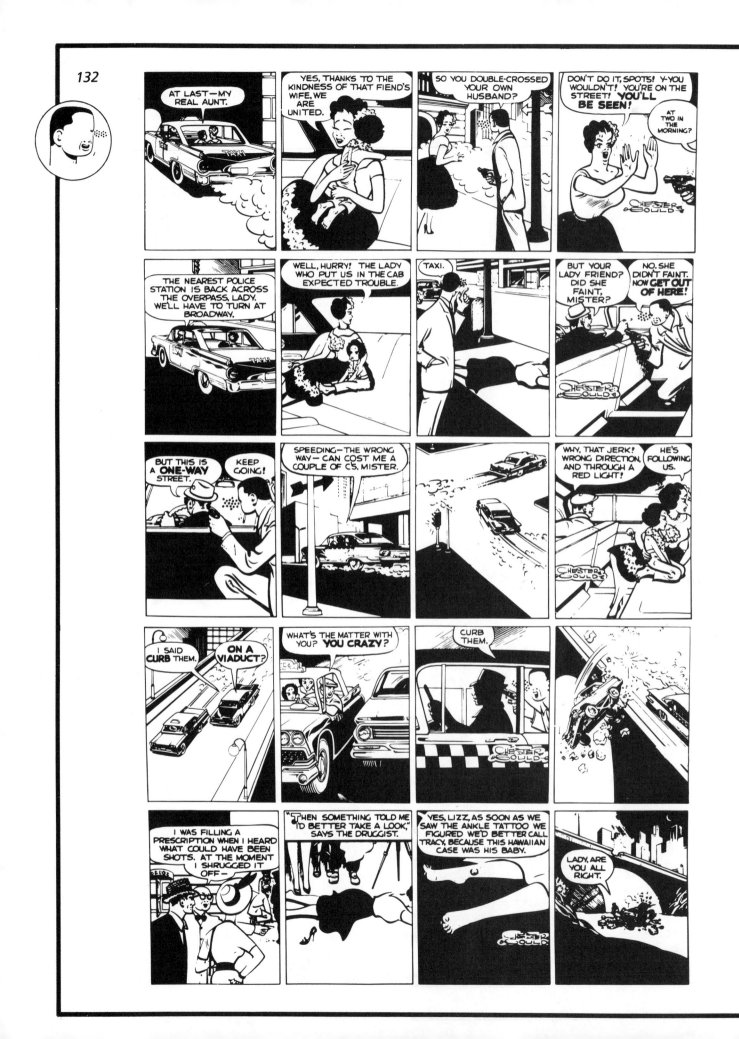

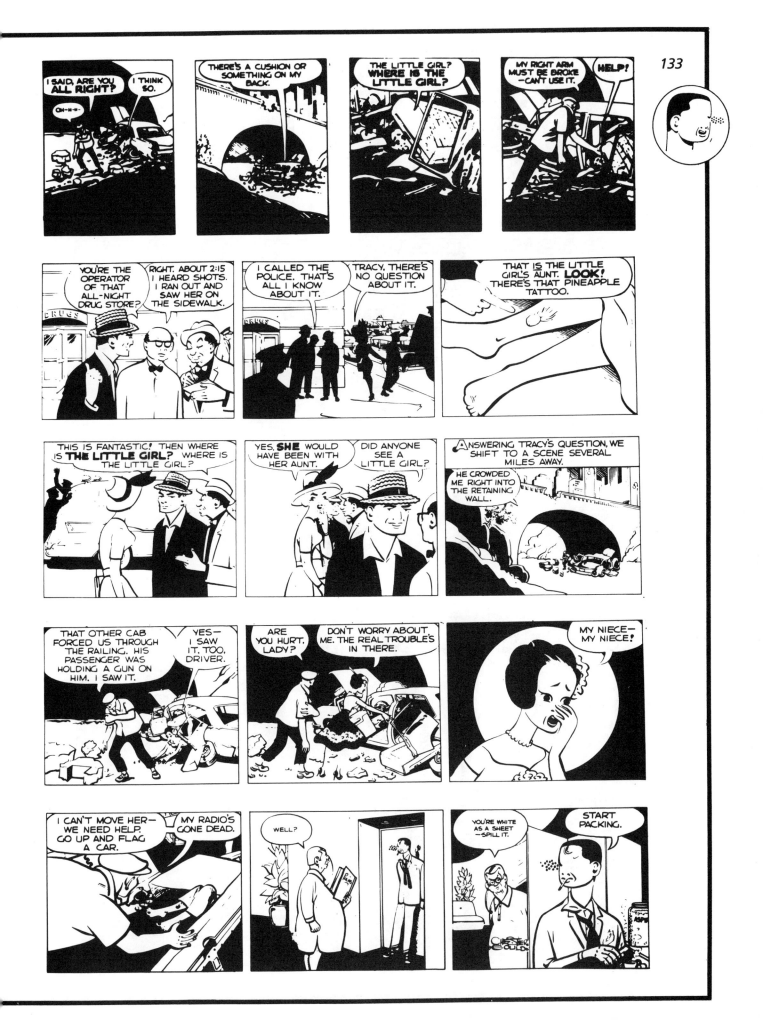

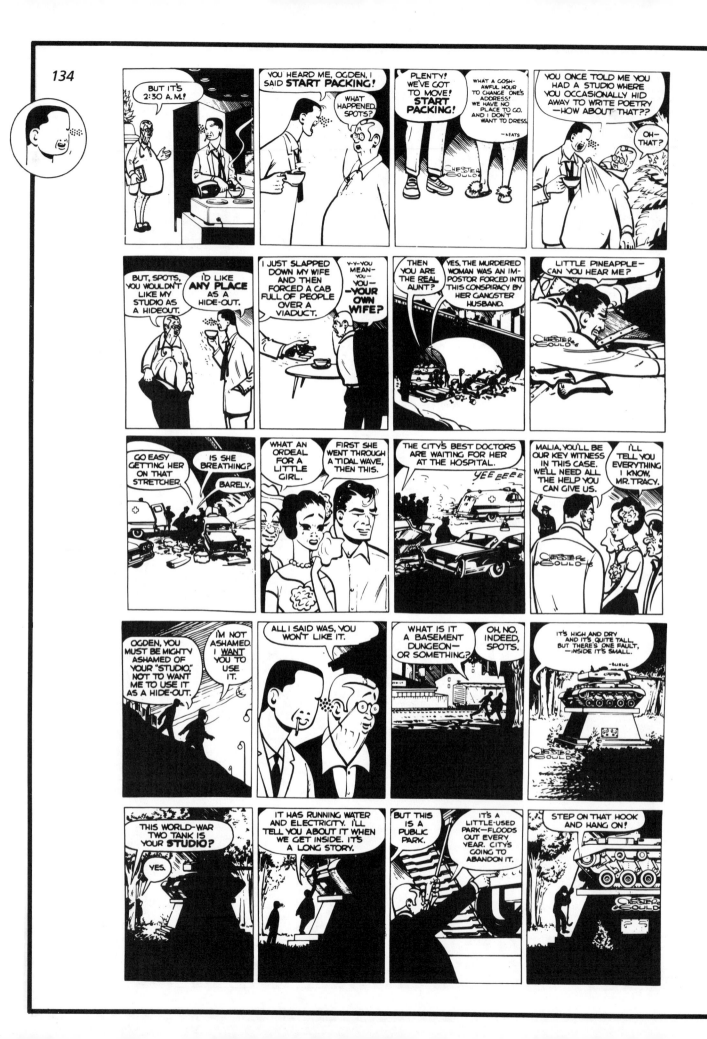

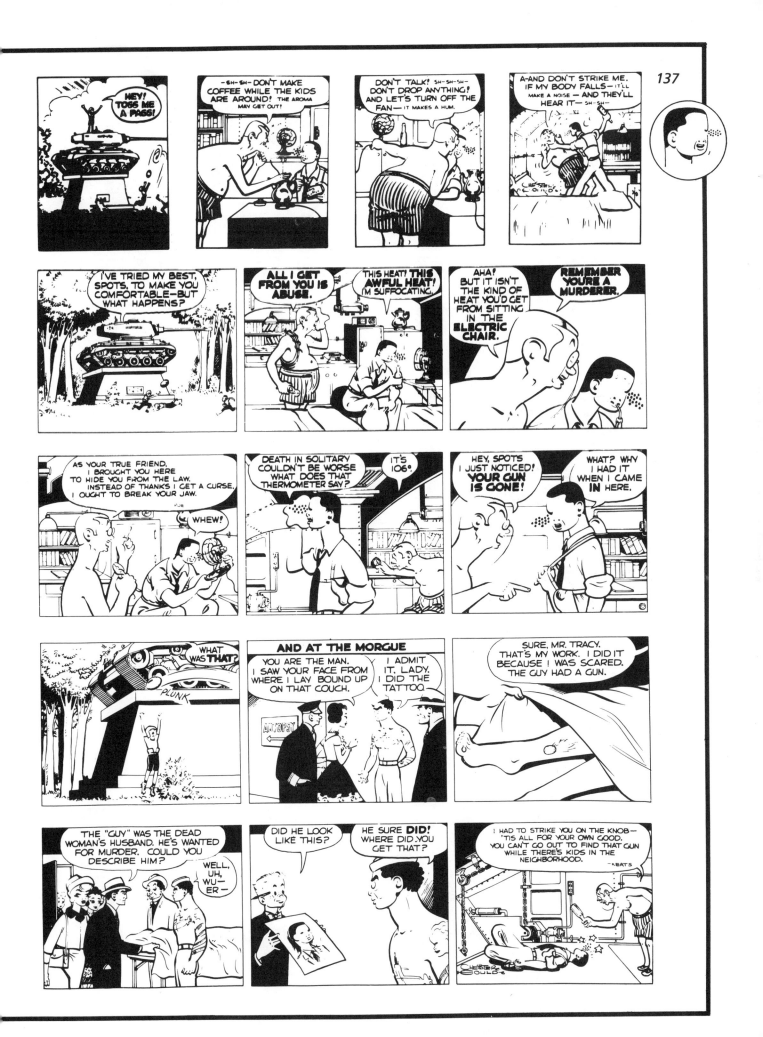

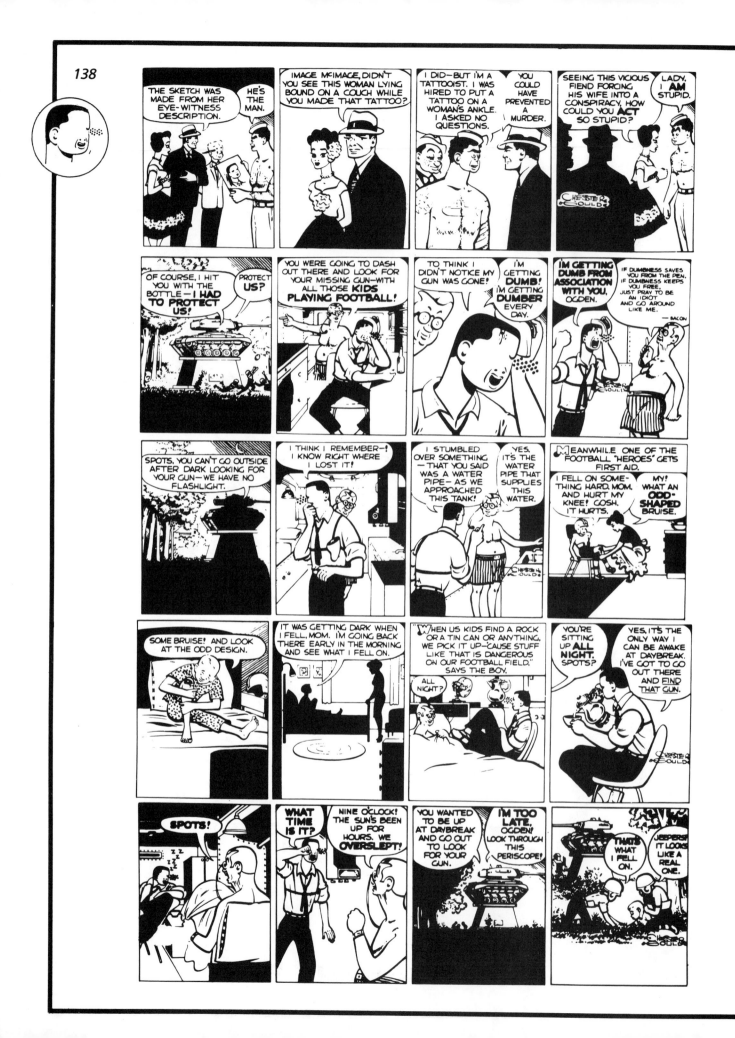

139

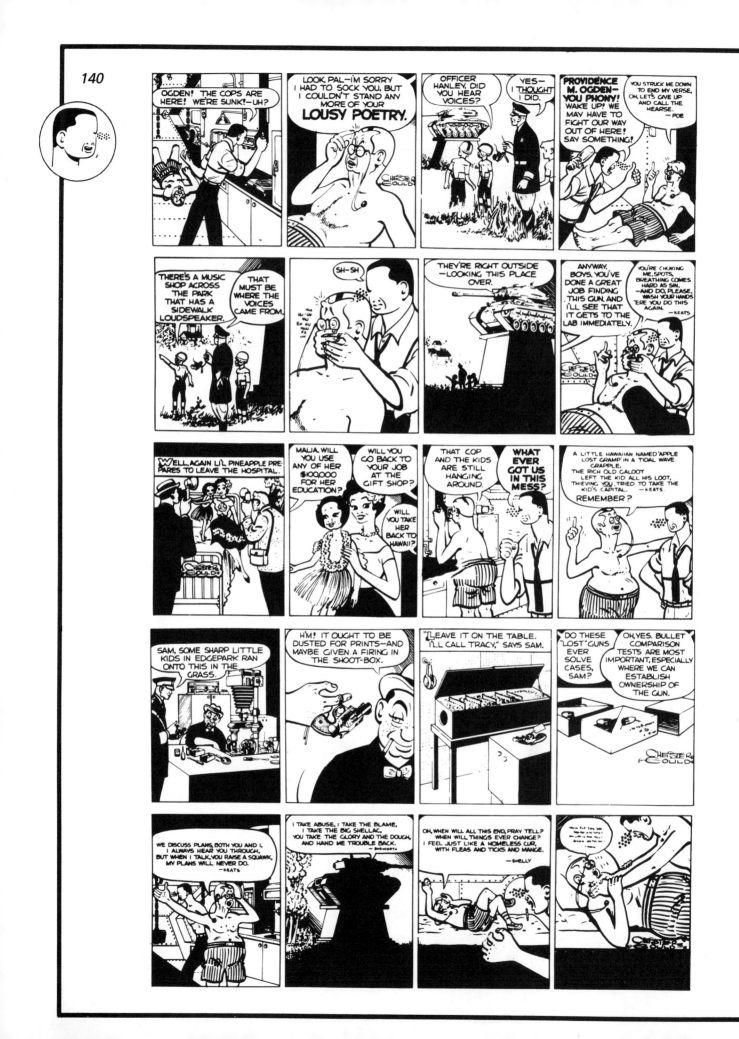

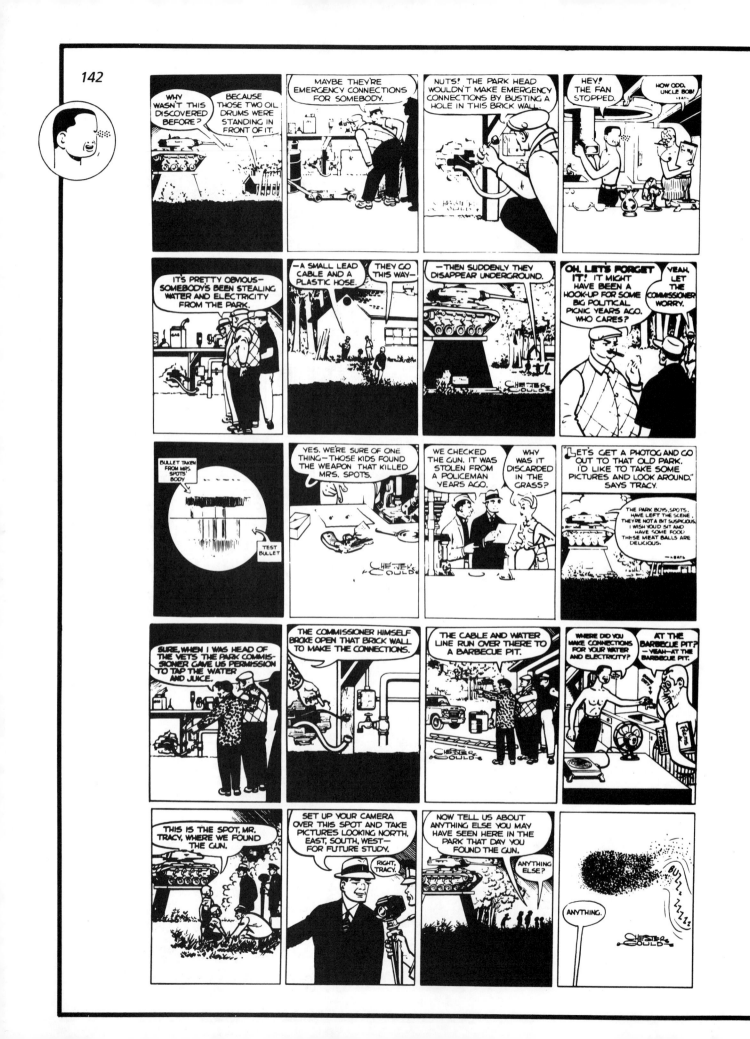

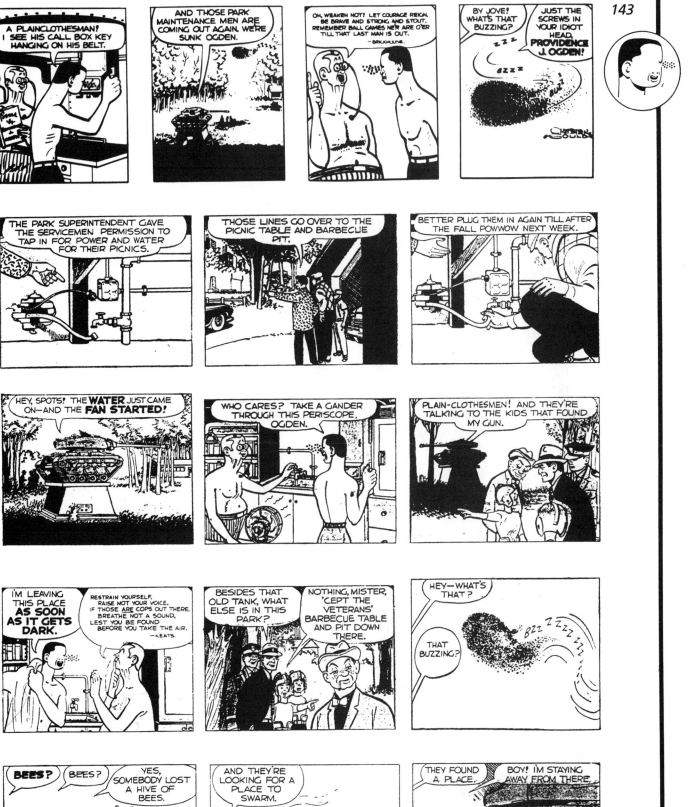

143

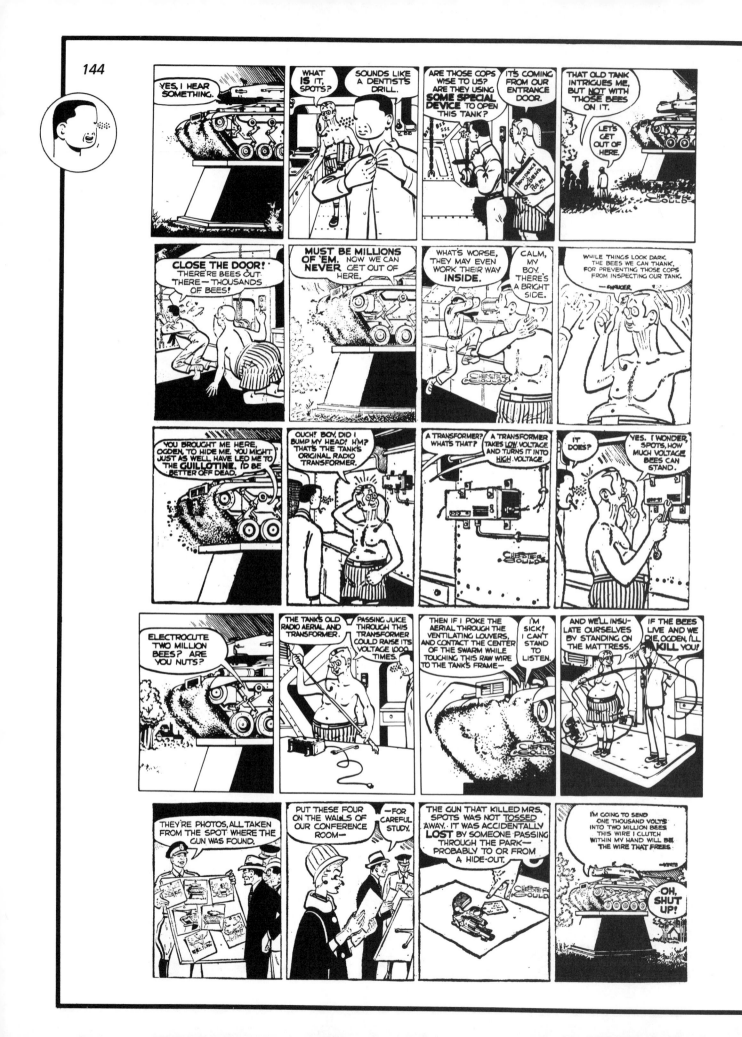

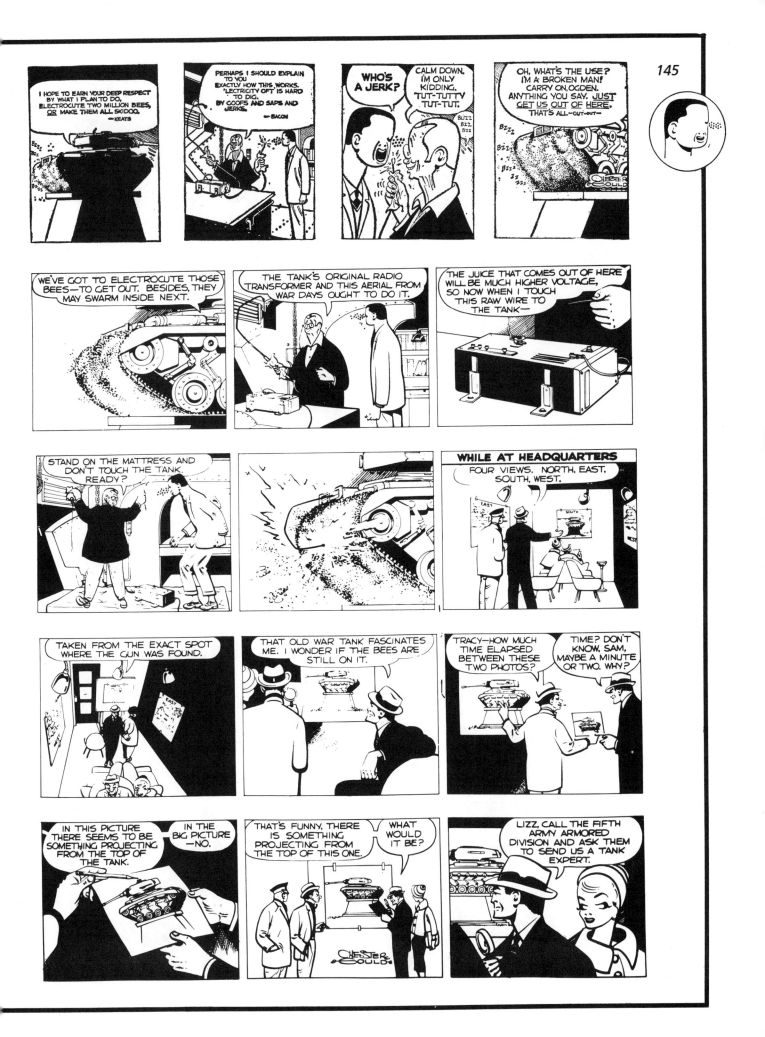

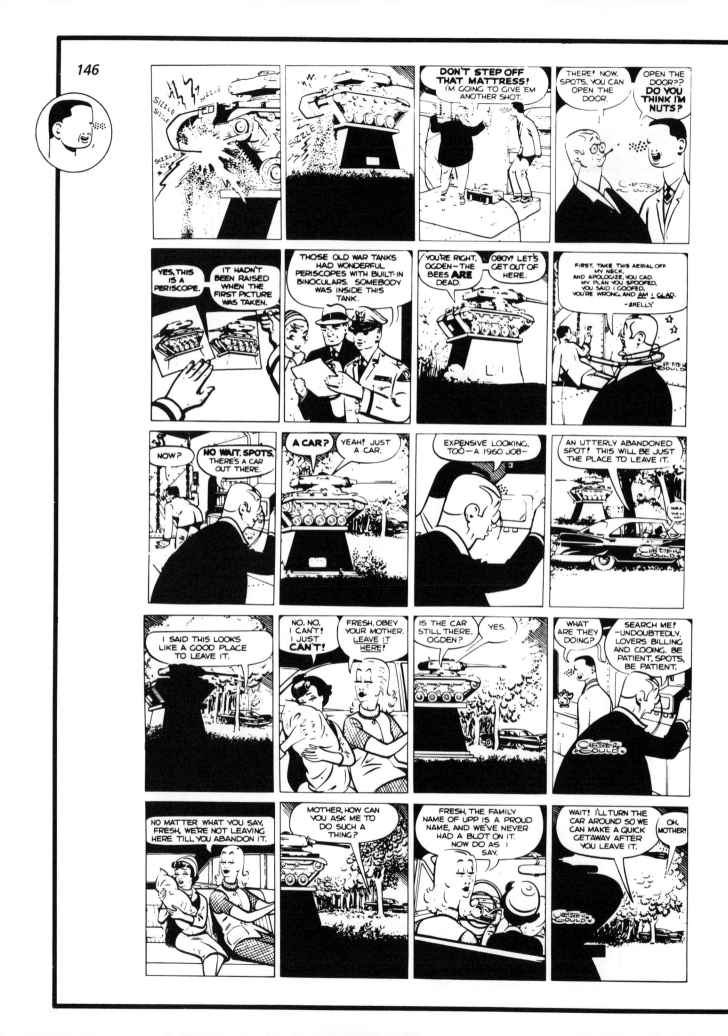

147

148

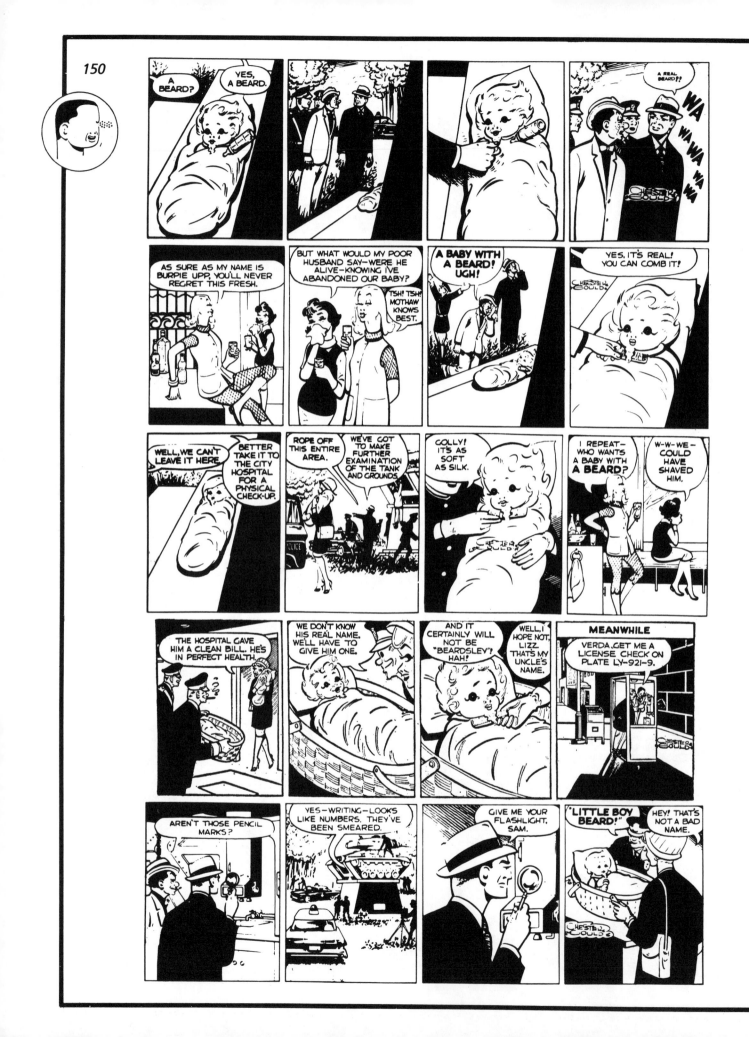

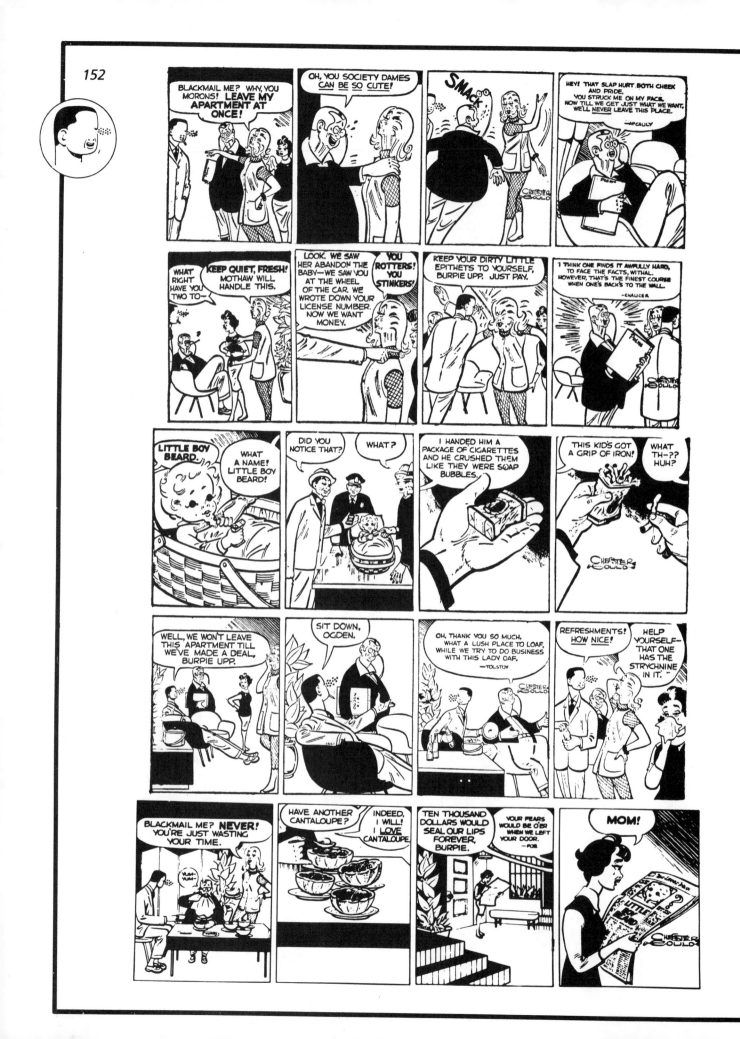

153

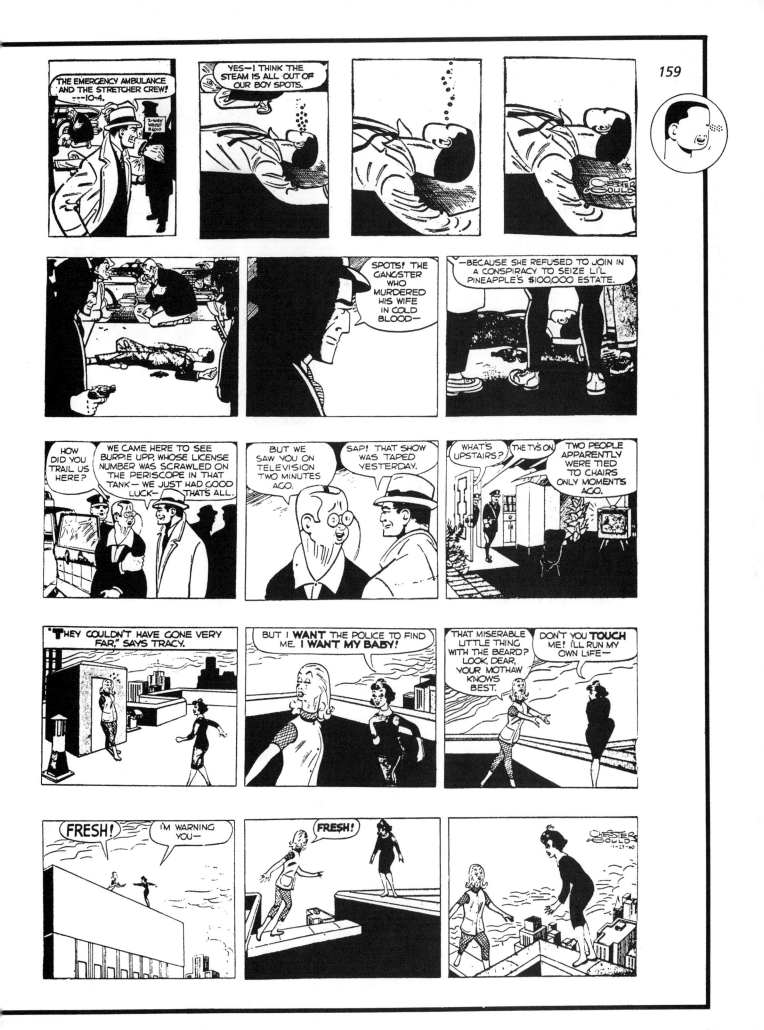

THE 1970s
BIG BOY'S OPEN CONTRACT
by Max Allan Collins and Rick Fletcher
6/12/78–12/30/78

Chester Gould's final years on *Tracy* were marked by continued artistic excellence. The artwork slipped somewhat, however, from the superb sixties visuals, especially when the Tribune Syndicate handed Gould a new Sunday page format in 1974, forcing him to abandon the full-page tabloid-style originals he'd done since 1931 in favor of a smaller half-page format.

If the stories still suffered from a tendency to meander, the moon sequences had all but disappeared (despite Moon Maid's continued occasional presence) and there was a refreshing infusion of topical material—record counterfeiting, obscene phone calls, a feminist bank robbery ring, a Watergate-style crooked politician. A last burst of strong villains included the Button, Pucker Puss, and the Pouch. A rather unfortunate attempt by Gould to make Tracy seem up-to-date resulted in an unflattering longer hairstyle and a mustache that was wholly inappropriate—a fact that Gould came to recognize, as seen when the regular cast eventually held Tracy down for an enforced shave!

In 1977 Gould retired, and turned the artistic reins over to his longtime assistant Rick Fletcher. The coeditor of this volume, Max Allan Collins, was selected to write the strip after submitting a sample story ("Dick Tracy Meets Angeltop"), which became the new team's first continuity. For a time, Gould's name remained on the strip (with Collins and Fletcher); but Chet's only role was that of informal consultant to the writer.

The continuity included here—a long two-part one, actually—is the third Collins/Fletcher offering. It was the writer's wish to bring the strip full circle, providing, finally, a conclusion to the very first story: the return, and eventual demise, of Big Boy.

Also, although the moon had played an increasingly small role in Chester Gould's universe, writer Collins wished to send a message to the editors and readers by removing, once and for all, that aspect of the story—making it clear that Dick Tracy operated not out of a flying magnetic bucket, but a squad car; bringing the strip solidly back to earth. Rather than simply pretending the moon sequence had never happened, the *Tracy* continuity addressed it head-on with the violent removal of a sympathetic character (a long-standing Gould tradition).

The fan mail ran strongly in favor of the removal of this character, incidentally, although a vocal few continue to express their dissenting votes.

Additionally, a parallel subplot was designed to get the Sparkle Plenty character back on track—and in a position to eventually marry Junior Tracy—through the departure of her cartoonist husband Vera Alldid (an uninspired Gould creation of the seventies) by way of an offstage divorce. The bittersweet love affair between Sparkle and a hitman was an effort to invoke the poignance of the Model/Junior tragedy.

One of the reasons this story was chosen for inclusion here is the strength of Fletcher's artwork. While Rick did a craftsmanlike job throughout his run on the strip, it's generally agreed that his first year or so represents his finest work—crisp, modern, and sufficiently Gould-like, without smothering Fletcher's native, rather more illustrative style.

165

173

TRACY MEETS WITH INSPECTOR PRICE, ORGANIZED CRIME UNIT...

BIG BOY? YES, HE'S STILL AN APPARATUS MEMBER. PRETTY INACTIVE.

STILL, HE'S ON THE EXECUTIVE COUNCIL. WE'RE BUILDING A CASE AGAINST HIM AND OTHER MEMBERS, NOW. BUT HE WON'T STAND TRIAL.

WHY?

HE'LL BE DEAD. DOCTORS GIVE HIM SIX MONTHS...

HMMM.

WE KNOW TWO MINOR APPARATUS HOODS WERE SPREADIN' THE WORD ABOUT THE $1,000,000 OPEN CONTRACT...

SO IT FIGURES AN APPARATUS BIG SHOT PUT OUT THE CONTRACT.

BUT WHY DO YOU THINK IT'S BIG BOY? OLD-TIMER LIKE THAT...

THAT'S PART OF THE REASON.

TODAY'S APPARATUS KEEPS A LOWER PROFILE THAN THIS $1,000,000 BOUNTY SUGGESTS. HAS TO BE A REVENGE—HAPPY "OLD-TIMER" AS YOU PUT IT.

AND BIG BOY'S AN "OLD-TIME" GANGSTER WITH A $1,000,000 WORTH OF GRUDGE AGAINST TRACY.

LAB GOT SOMETHING FOR US, AL?

YES—WE'VE STUDIED THE PATH OF THE EXPLOSION—

"IT'S APPARENT THE BOMB WAS WIRED IN UNDER THE DASH—NOT THE HOOD."

"EXPLAINS HOW IT MIGHT'VE BEEN DONE QUICKLY ENOUGH TO GET BY A COP ON GUARD," TRACY SAYS.

WE BLEW IT.

NOW, NOW... WE'LL JUST TRY AGAIN.

188

192

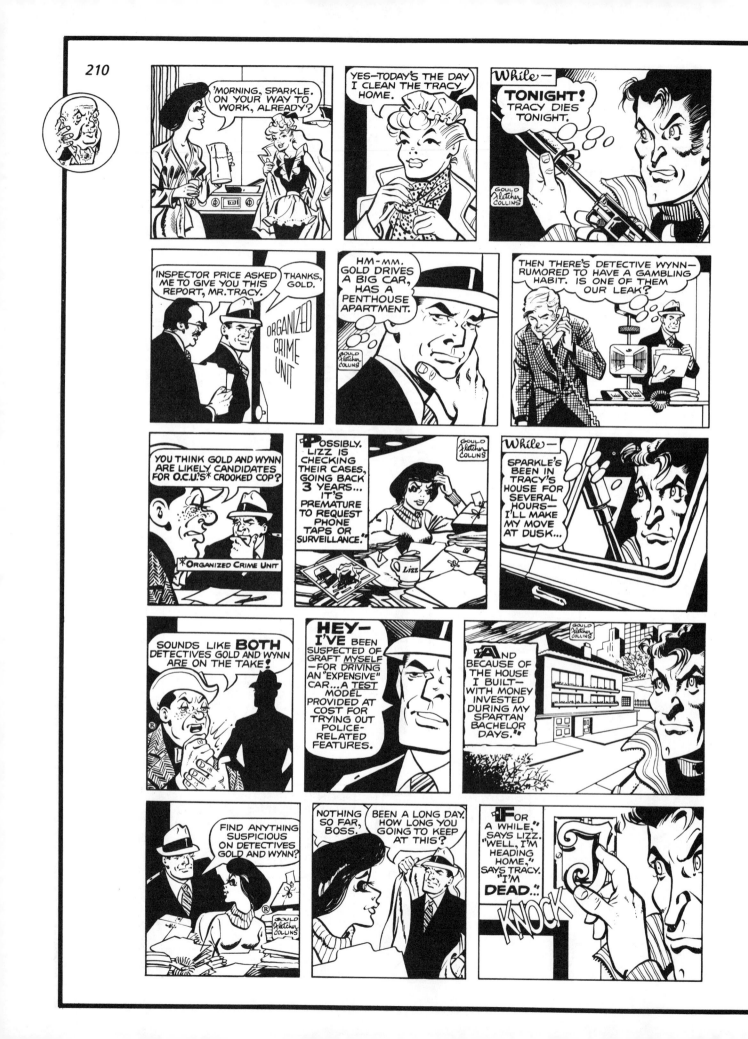

212

213

THE 1980s
THE MAN OF A MILLION FACES
by Max Allan Collins and Dick Locher
10/5/87–4/10/88

The late seventies and the 1980s have seen *Dick Tracy* deal with an increasing list of modern crimes. Video piracy, inner city arson, corporate kidnapping, computer viruses, product tampering, toxic waste dumping, police corruption, stock market fraud, skyjacking, international terrorism and black market adoption are among the crimes the classic detective has tackled. Tracy has traveled to Moscow, the Caribbean, and all around his native U.S.A. Technology has manifested itself in holograms, nuclear fusion, and a Two-Way Wrist Computer.

The basic cast has remained intact, although black policewoman Lee Ebony has joined Tracy's Major Crime Squad (another character, the young, mustached Johnny Adonis, was aboard for several years, as well). Policewoman Lizz married fellow Officer Groovy Grove, only to be widowed shortly thereafter. Dick and Tess have had another child, young Joe, and Junior and Sparkle have (at last!) married, and have a lovely young offspring—Sparkle Plenty, Jr.

After the untimely death of Rick Fletcher in 1983, Dick Locher returned to *Tracy* as artist, assisted by his talented son John. While the emphasis remains on topical crime, the Collins/Locher period is marked by a return to more humor (with frequent appearances by Vitamin Flintheart and B.O. Plenty and Gravel Gertie) and villains in the grand Gould grotesque style.

For all of the above talk of topicalilty, the editors have chosen, as a representative of their own work, a story about a mere bank robber.

But "mere" is perhaps not the correct word to describe the Man of a Million Faces, a.k.a. Putty Puss.

Locher and Collins agree that Putty Puss is their favorite villain to date—and the one most like a classic Gould villain. Collins admits the inspiration for this character comes at least partially from Anyface, a villain in the spoof "Fearless Fosdick" (the strip-within-a-strip parody of *Tracy* that ran for years in Al Capp's *Li'l Abner*). Because Putty Puss can assume the faces of others, political cartoonist Locher's ability to caricature the famous and infamous of our times often came into play in this continuity.

Also, Tracy ultimately finds himself in a death trap of which Gould might well have approved. While the crimes in today's *Dick Tracy* may be new, some things never change, and dreaming up fantastic scrapes for Tracy to think himself out of is a basic tenet of the Chester Gould canon.

Coeditor Collins must peek out from behind the third-person facade to report what a delight it is to work with a gifted cartoonist like Dick Locher; his touch for humor as well as his striking black-and-white sense, which rivals Gould's own, are assets to the strip that cannot be underestimated. Collins feels lucky to have been able to work with two men who trained at the elbow of the master himself; without Fletcher and Locher to give a sense of continuity between the Gould and post-Gould periods, *Tracy* might be less "legitimate" a continuation of a classic strip. Predictions that Gould—like Walt Kelly, George Herriman, and Al Capp—would be an impossible act to follow have not proven accurate. Hard, yes; impossible, no.

On the other hand, the editors of this book are the first to say that they will never approach even the vaguest outskirts of Chester Gould at his best.

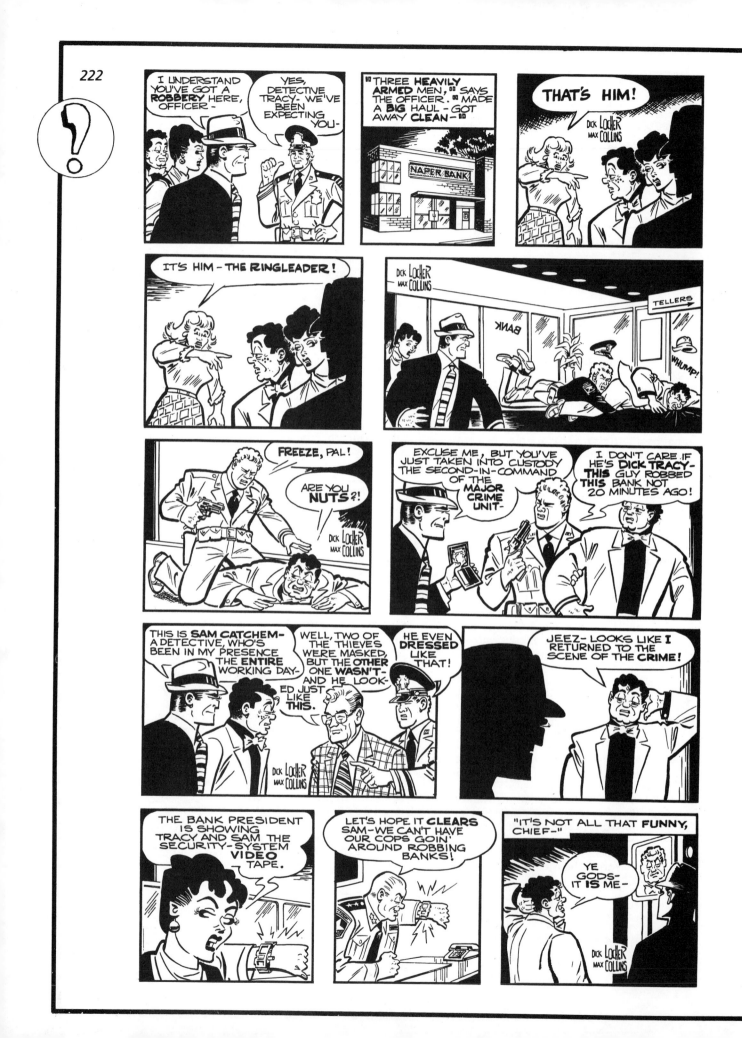

223

228

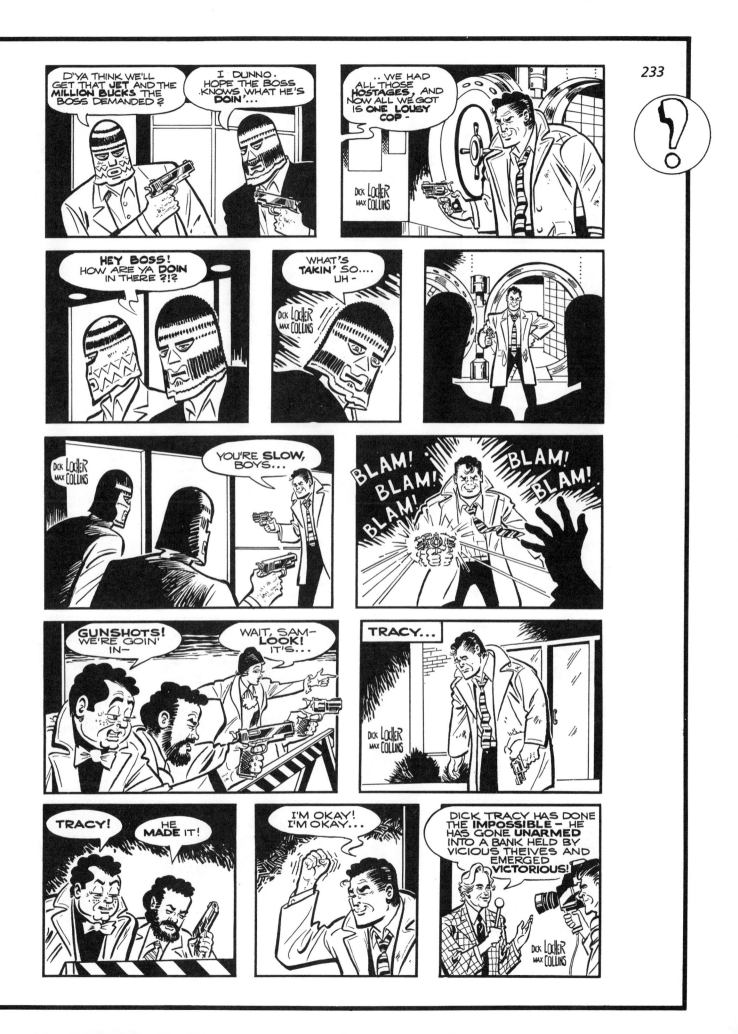

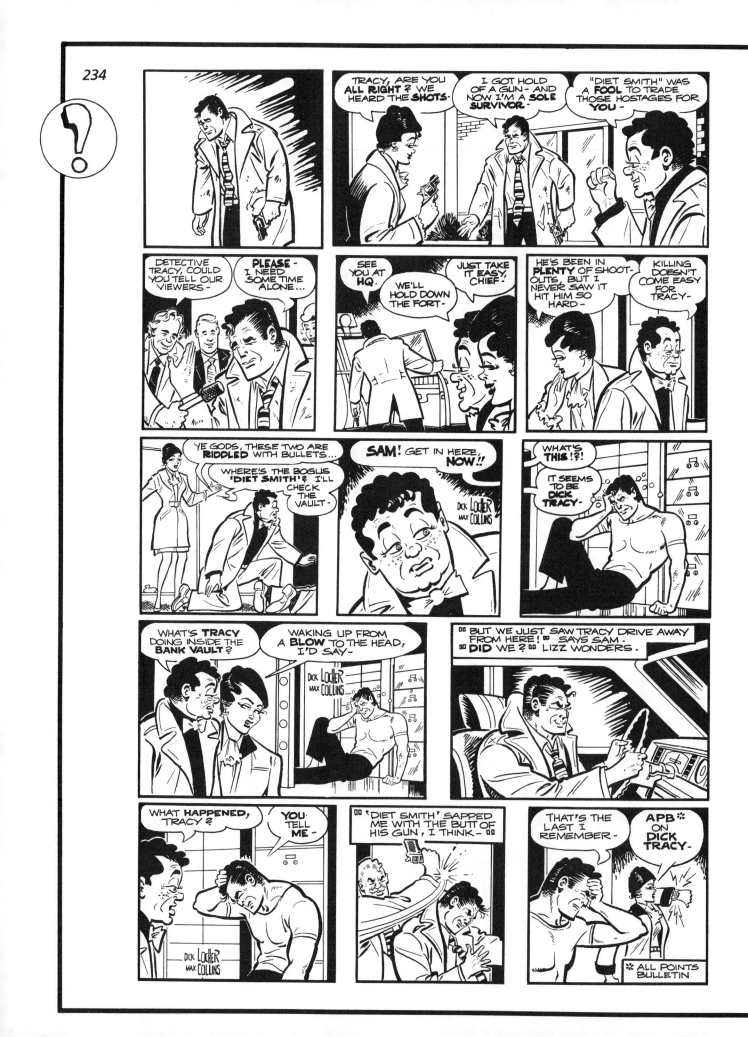

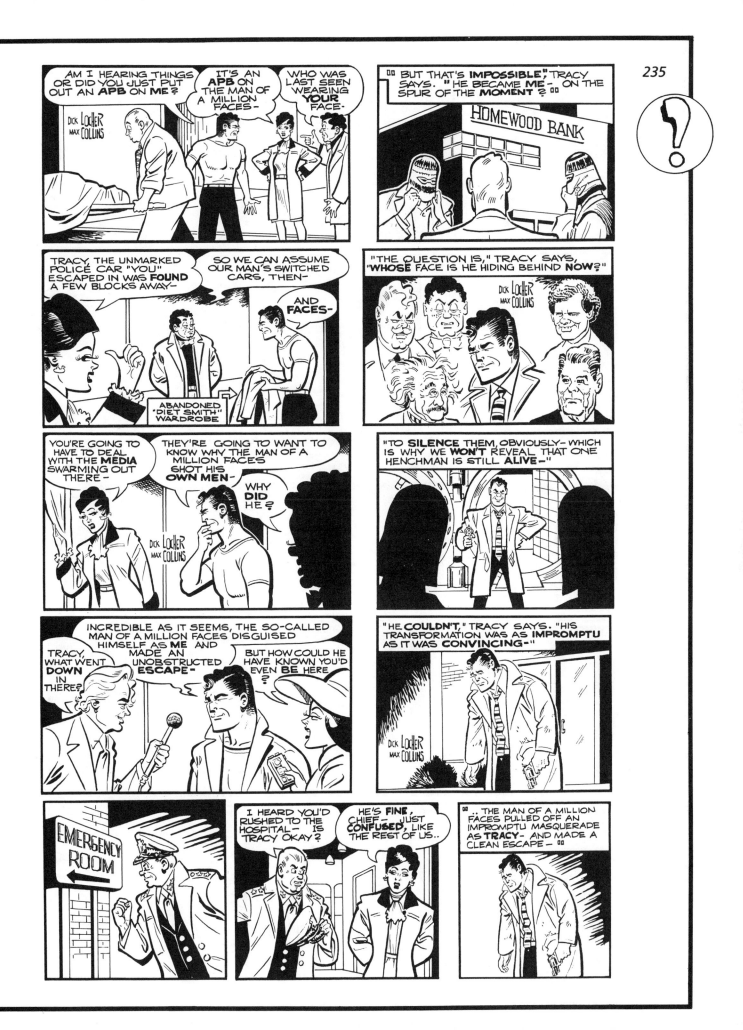

236

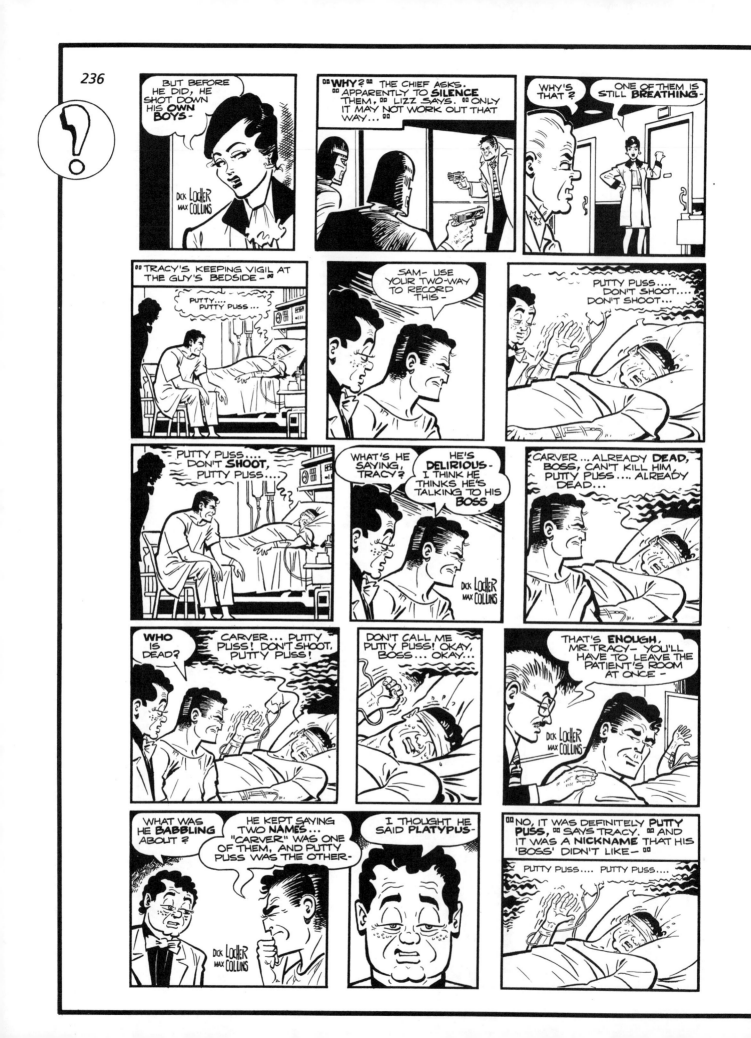

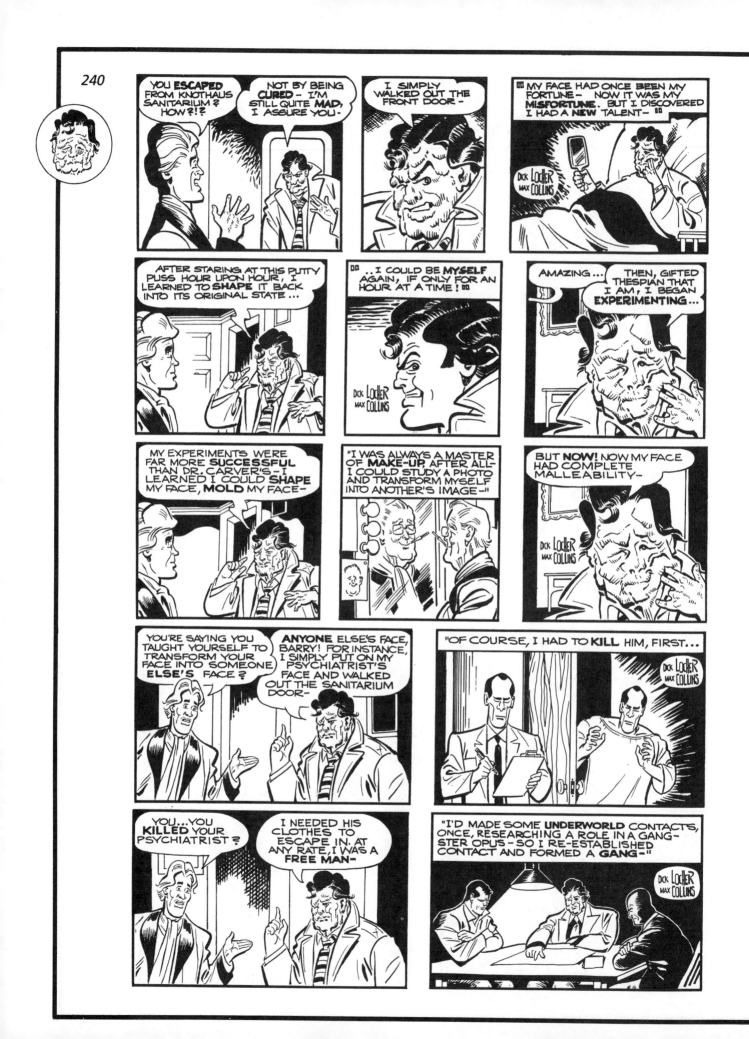

253

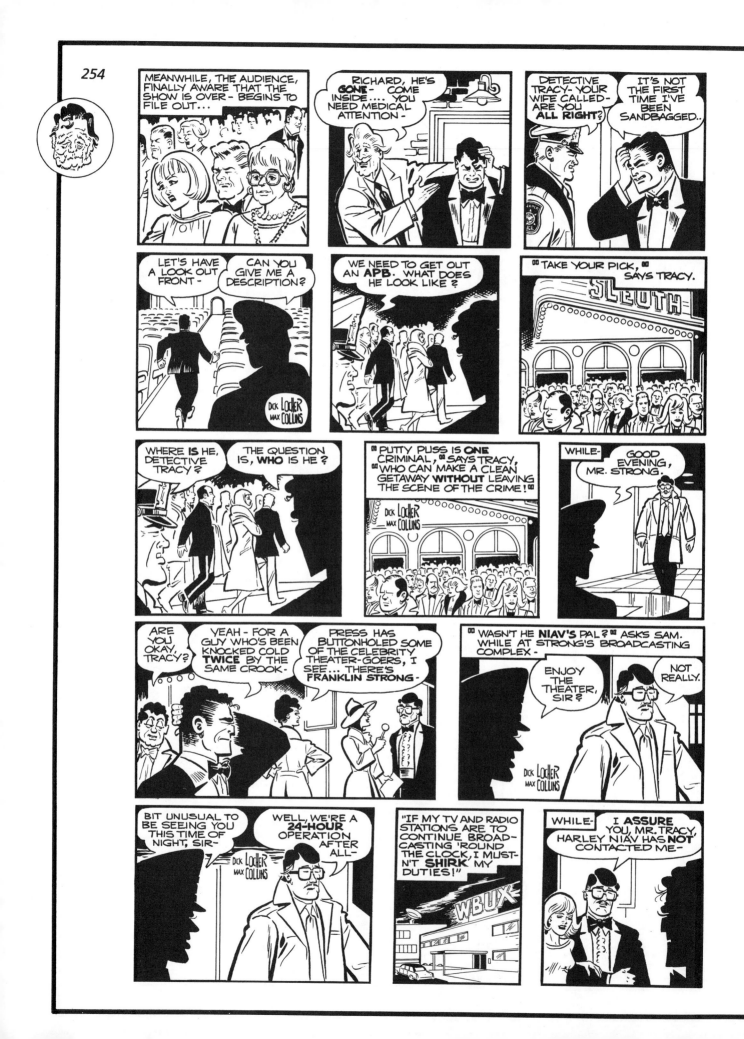

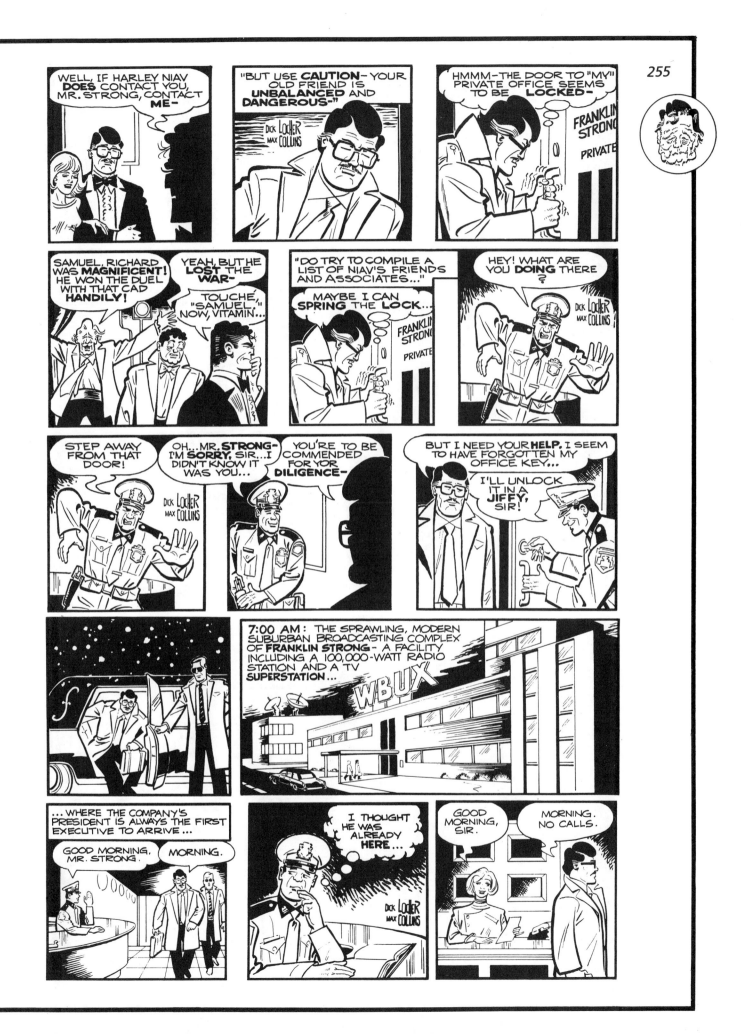

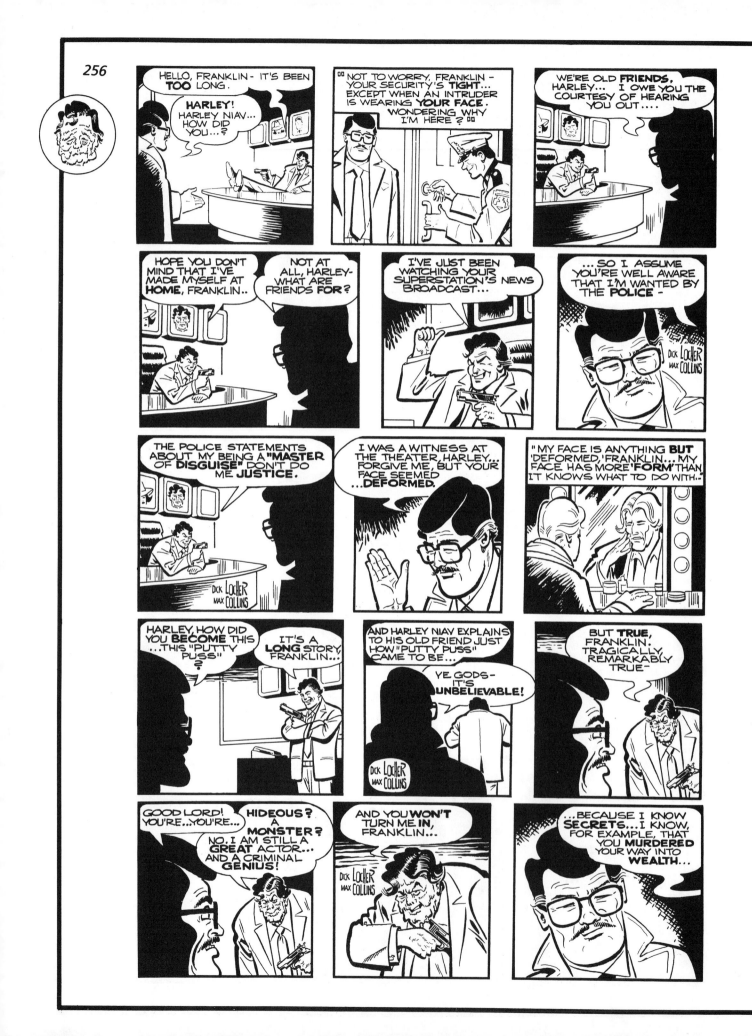

259

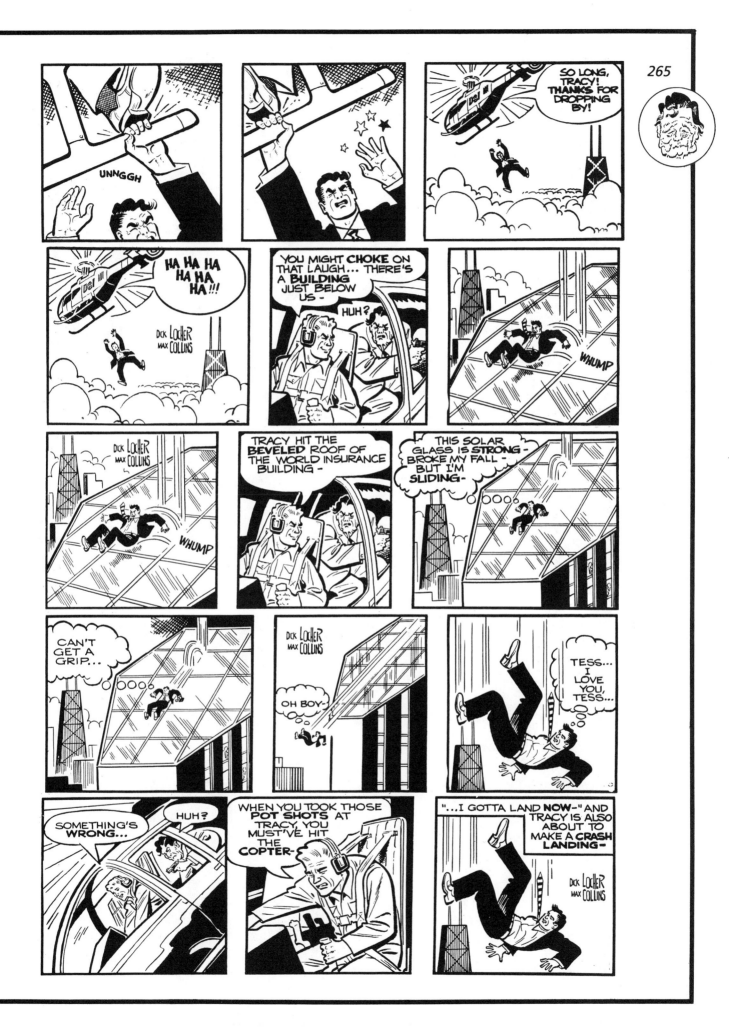

A SIX-YEAR-OLD REMEMBERS:
An Afterword

I was six years old, I would guess, when I first encountered *Dick Tracy*.

I'd begun to read comic books—the Carl Barks *Donald Duck* and *Uncle Scrooge* and the Wayne Boring *Superman*—and had been read nightly doses of Edgar Rice Burroughs' *Tarzan* by my mother for some time. It was my mom who prompted me to try *Dick Tracy*—considering that *Parents* magazine listed *Tracy* as one of the most violent and objectionable comic books around, it's lucky I had the mom I did. She had read the *Tracy* strip faithfully during the war, when my dad was a navy officer stationed in San Diego. She knew what an exciting, wonderful strip it was.

So I used my ten-cent weekly allowance to buy *Dick Tracy* #79. As I mentioned obliquely above, I read not the strip, but the *Tracy* comic books, which were published by Harvey Comics, and which collected the newspaper strip in slightly edited, four-color form. We did not have the *Tracy* strip in our local paper and it took several years for me to cajole my father into buying the Sunday Chicago *Tribune* so that I could follow my favorite sleuth.

Several of the stories in this book represent the first *Tracy* stories I ever read. They shaped me as a person, specifically shaped me as a writer; the kind of stories I write (and this extends to my novels, not just *Dick Tracy* and other comics writing), and the approach I take with those stories, flow from three tales collected in this volume.

Just as it was a dream come true to write *Dick Tracy*, it is now a dream come true to see these three stories gathered in one volume, particularly one with my name on it, and one that includes several *Tracy* stories of my own!

The first *Tracy* story I read was "The Case of the Parking Meter Bandits." This was the story that you've already read (and if you're reading this Afterword first, *stop*—go back and read the stories first!), in which Model Jones and Junior Tracy fall in love. I was spellbound by the interwoven tale of a detective tracking down petty thieves, not knowing that his own son was courting the sweet sister of the bandits' ringleader. The heartbreaking scene that has Model pretending to reject Junior brought tears to my young eyes—and it still does, frankly, when I allow it to.

But here's where Chet Gould first fried my brain; where he first twisted me, and my perceptions of life and storytelling. . . .

Issue #79 ended just after Larry's bullet goes twirling through his poor sister's body.

That was the cliffhanger, kids.

Six-year-old Al Collins waited for a month to see how that would resolve, confident, of course, that all would be right with the world when #80 appeared on a rack at Cohn's News; that Model would survive and she (if not she and Junior) would live happily ever after.

Well, that month passed, and issue #80 arrived, and Model died. ("It hurts," she said, in an eloquently simple, tragic panel.) She was dead. She was real dead. She was very, very dead. Dead dead. And I was one fried six-year-old. I didn't know from death, in the comics or anywhere else. I was very disturbed by this. I'm sure social do-gooders and child psychologists would be equally disturbed about a six-year-old being so disturbed. To hell with them.

I loved it. Instinctively, I knew something very special had happened; that a story—a made-up story—had touched me deeply.

I scrambled around to secondhand shops and to a tiny nearby mom-and-pop market where the comics (like the milk) stayed on sale long past the recommended time, and scrounged up the preceding several issues of *Dick Tracy*. These reprinted the Crewy Lou story as "The Case of the Fiendish Photographers." The action here, particularly the sequence on the wharf, when the bullets really fly, was similarly brain-frying. Such moments as Sphinx getting crushed by the elevator, Sam hurling the wad of money in King's face, and Crewy Lou being threatened by her brother Brainerd, were like electric shocks to my brain. And when Bonnie Braids was in danger, I knew she was in *danger*—this guy Gould was capable of killing her off!

That, incidentally, is what the Model story taught me about crime fiction: you must kill off a sympathetic character now and then, to remind readers that they are in an unstable world, where anything can happen. Sure, Dick Tracy isn't going to die; but *anybody else* in his world just might! (I regret that the Tribune Media Services editors, several years ago, would not allow me to kill off Chief Pat Patton. I was after just this sort of shock to the reader's system.)

The next story I read was *really* disturbing. My aunt Oma, knowing of my burgeoning love for Tracy, picked up (on a sale table at Younkers Department Store in Des Moines, Iowa) a copy of a rare little item called *The Exploits of Dick Tracy*, "The Case of the Brow." If my brain was already sizzling on the griddle of Chester Gould's imagination, old Chet pressed down on me hard, now, with his spatula. . . .

I encountered the sexy, naughty Summer Sisters, who had to endure the Brow's spike machine (!), little droplets of blood pearling their shapely legs. I of course encountered the Brow himself, the sadist who stuck those limbs into that spike machine, in which he eventually found his own head stuck when the Summer Sisters took their revenge. Later in the story, I witnessed Tracy himself struck with a spearlike lightning rod, our hero actually going to hospital to recover, something heroes had never done in any other stories I'd thus far encountered. And finally I saw the Brow get impaled on a flag pole, meeting a Nazi spy's just if grisly reward.

Most of all, though, I had seen the Brow take his revenge on the Summer Sisters; when the girls, underwater in a car forced off a bridge, seemed to drown, I kept turning pages, waiting for them somehow to come miraculously back to life. They didn't, of course. After Model Jones, I should have known. Studying Gould's panel of the drowned girls, I should also have known 'cause nobody drew dead people like Chet. Their shapely limbs askew, their eyes shut, their bodies floating, the Summer Sisters—despite the smallness of their sins—had paid a large price.

As I continued to collect *Tracy* comics— and Big Little Books, when I could find them

(the story adapted to BLB as "From Colorado to Nova Scotia" would have been in this volume, if it hadn't been reprinted relatively recently in *Dick Tracy: The Thirties*, Chelsea House, 1978)—I began to write and draw my own stories. I wanted to be a cartoonist, and of course my scribblings were mostly of Dick Tracy. My mother, without my knowledge, gathered some of these drawings and sent them to Chester Gould. He did something very special for me, something that literally changed my life: He wrote me a letter congratulating me on my recent eighth birthday, and told me I drew Tracy better than anybody else my age. Actually, Tracy himself told me, in a drawing Chet made.

It was the biggest thrill of my life, to that date, and few thrills since have come close to matching it.

I wrote Chet back and thanked him, and asked him if I could take over the strip when he retired. He rewarded my audacity with another letter. He was extremely kind to me.

As I grew older, my interest in *Dick Tracy* extended to crime and mystery fiction in general. It takes no great leap of the imagination to see how the six-year-old me, loving *Dick Tracy*, could become the thirteen-year-old me, sitting devouring *One Lonely Night* by Mickey Spillane. At some point in junior high, I stopped wanting to be a cartoonist and started wanting to be a mystery writer.

But I never stopped loving *Dick Tracy* and its creator. That was the difference between me and most kids who liked *Tracy*. Most of them fantasized about being Dick Tracy. I fantasized about being Chester Gould. I knew, from that distinctive signature on the covers of the comic books, that somebody was responsible for those wonderful stories.

I wanted to be somebody like that. I wanted to give six-year-olds, of all ages, wonderful stories. I hope, in some small degree, in both my novels and my comics work, that I've succeeded in that goal.

MAX ALLAN COLLINS
November 1, 1989

WOODSTOCK — ILLINOIS

HI ALLAN

Dear Allan: I have lots of
friends, but none that
can draw my picture,
at your age, any better
than you. Your mother
sent me a drawing
you made and its a
wow! Many thanks
far thinking of me.
Oh yes — you were 8
years old Saturday and
I want to say now
Happy Birthday!
Sorry I'm late!
As ever
Dick Tracy
and
CHESTER GOULD